The Children's Treasury of Animal Stories

The Children's Treasury of

ANIMAL STORIES

Edited by Anne Roberts
Illustrated by Jan Machalek

KEY PORTER BOOKS

Toronto

CANADIAN CATALOGUING IN PUBLICATION DATA

Main entry under title:
The Children's treasury of animal stories
ISBN 1-55013-504-X

1. Animals — Juvenile literature. I. Roberts, Anne.
II. Machalek, Jan.

PZ5.C5   j398.24'52   C93-094234-5

Key Porter Books Limited
70 The Esplanade
Toronto, ON
M5E 1R2

Contributing editor: Anne Roberts
Illustration: Jan Machalek
Typesetting: MacTrix DTP

Printed and bound in Spain

93 94 95 96 5 4 3 2 1

CONTENTS

The Children's Treasury of

ANIMAL STORIES

THE GREAT SEA SERPENT

HANS CHRISTIAN ANDERSEN

There once was a little fish. He was of good family; his name I have forgotten—if you want to know it, you must ask someone learned in these matters. He had one thousand and eight hundred brothers and sisters, all born at the same time. They did not know their parents and had to take care of themselves. They swam around happily in the sea. They had enough water to drink—all the great oceans of the world. They did not speculate upon where their food would come from, that would come by itself. Each wanted to follow his own inclinations and live his own life; not that they gave much thought to that either.

The sun shone down into the sea and illuminated the water. It was a strange world, filled with the most fantastic creatures; some of them were so big and had such huge jaws that they could have swallowed all eighteen hundred of the little fish at once. But this, too, they did not worry about, for none of them had been eaten yet.

The little fishes swam close together, as herring or mackerel do. They were thinking about nothing except swimming. Suddenly they heard a terrible noise, and from the surface of the sea a great thing was cast among them.

There was more and more of it; it was endless and had neither head nor tail. It was heavy and every one of the small fishes that it hit was either stunned and thrown aside or had its back broken.

The fishes—big and small, the ones who lived up near the waves and those who dwelled in the depths—all fled, while this monstrous serpent grew longer and longer as it sank deeper and deeper, until at last it was hundreds of miles long, and lay at the bottom of the sea, crossing the whole ocean.

All the fishes—yes, even the snails and all the other animals that live in the sea—saw or heard about the strange, gigantic, unknown eel that had descended into the sea from the air above.

What was it? We know that it was the telegraph cable, thousands of miles long, that human beings had laid to connect America and Europe.

All the inhabitants of the sea were frightened of this new huge animal that had come to live among them. The flying fishes leaped up from the sea and into the air; and the gurnard since it knew how, shot up out of the water like a bullet. Others went down into the depths of the ocean so fast that they were there before the telegraph cable. They frightened both the cod and the flounder, who were swimming around peacefully, hunting and eating their fellow creatures.

A couple of sea cucumbers were so petrified that they spat out their own stomachs in fright; but they survived, for they knew how to swallow them again. Lots of lobsters and crabs left their shells in the confusion. During all this, the eighteen hundred little fishes were separated; most of them never saw one another again, nor would they have recognized one another if they had. Only a dozen of them stayed in the same spot, and after they had lain still a couple of hours their worst fright was over and curiosity became stronger than fear.

They looked about, both above and below themselves, and there at the bottom of the sea they thought they saw the monster that had frightened them all. It looked thin, but who knew how big it could make itself or how strong it was. It lay very still, but it might be up to something.

The more timid of the small fish said, "Let it lie where it is, it is no concern of ours." But the tiniest of them were determined to find out what it was. Since the monster had come from above, it was better to seek information about it up there. They swam up to the surface of the ocean. The wind was still and the sea was like a mirror.

They met a dolphin. He is a fellow who likes to jump and to turn somersaults in the sea. The dolphin has eyes to see with and ought to have seen what happened, and therefore the little fishes approached it. But a dolphin only thinks about himself and his somersaults; he didn't know what to say, so he didn't say anything, but looked very proud.

A seal came swimming by just at that moment, and even though it eats small fishes, it was more polite than the dolphin. Luckily it happened to be full, and it knew more than the jumping fish. "Many a night have I lain on a wet stone—miles and miles away from here—and looked toward land, where live those treacherous creatures who call themselves, in their own language, men. They are always hunting me and my kind, though usually we manage to escape. That is exactly what happened to the great sea serpent that you are asking about—it got away from them. They had it in their power for ever so long, and kept it up on land. Now men wanted to transport it to another country, across the sea.—Why? you may ask, but I can't answer.—They had a lot of trouble getting it on board the ship. But they finally succeeded; after all, it was weakened from its stay on land. They rolled it up, round and round into a coil. It wiggled and writhed, and what a lot of noise it made! I heard it. When the ship got out to sea, the great eel slipped overboard. They tried to stop it. I saw them, there were dozens of hands holding onto its body. But they couldn't. Now it is lying down at the bottom of the sea, and I guess it will stay there for a while."

"It looks awfully thin," said the tiny fishes.

"They have starved it," explained the seal. "But it will soon get its old figure and strength back. I am sure it is the great sea serpent: the one men are so afraid of that they talk about it all the time. I had not believed it existed, but now I do. And that was it." With a flip of its tail, the seal dived and was gone.

"How much he knew and how well he talked," said one of the little fishes admiringly. "I have never known so much as I do now—I just hope it wasn't all lies."

"We could swim down and look," suggested the tiniest of the tiny fishes. "And on the way down we could hear what the other fishes think."

"We wouldn't move a fin to know anything more," said all the other tiny fishes, turned, and swam away.

"But I will," shouted the tiniest one, and swam down into the depths. But he was far away from where the great sea serpent had sunk. The little fish searched in every direction. Never had he realized that the world was so big.

Great shoals of herring glided by like silver boats, and behind them came schools of mackerel that were even more splendid and brilliant. There were fishes of all shapes, with all kinds of markings and colors. Jellyfish, looking like transparent plants, floated by, carried by the currents. Down at the bottom of the sea the strangest things grew: tall grasses and palm-shaped trees whose every leaf was covered with crustaceans.

At last the tiny fish spied a long dark line far below it and swam down to it. It was not the giant serpent but the railing of a sunken ship, whose upper and lower decks had been torn in two by the pressure of the sea. The little fish entered the great cabin, where the terrified passengers had gathered as the ship went down; they had all drowned and the currents of the sea had carried their bodies away, except for two of them: a young woman who lay on a bench with her babe in her arms. The sea rocked them gently; they looked as though they were sleeping. The little fish grew frightened as he looked at them. What if they were to wake? The cabin was so quiet and so lonely that the tiny fish hurried away again, out into the light, where there were other fishes. It had not swum very far when it met a young whale; it was awfully big.

"Please don't swallow me," pleaded the little fish. "I am so little you could hardly taste me, and I find it such a great pleasure to live."

"What are you doing down here?" grunted the whale. "It is much too deep for your kind." Then the tiny fish told the whale about the great eel—or whatever it could be—that had come from the air and descended into the sea, frightening even the most courageous fishes.

"Ha, ha, ha!" laughed the whale, and swallowed so

much water that it had to surface in order to breathe and spout the water out. "Ho-ho . . . ha-ha. That must have been the thing that tickled my back when I was turning over. I thought it was the mast of a ship and was just about to use it as a back scratcher; but it must have been that. It lies farther out. I think I will go and have a look at it; I haven't anything else to do."

The whale swam away and the tiny fish followed it, but not too closely for the great animal left a turbulent wake behind it.

They met a shark and an old sawfish. They, too, had heard about the strange great eel that was so thin and yet longer than any other fish. They hadn't seen it but wanted to.

A catfish joined them. "If that sea serpent is not thicker than an anchor cable, then I will cut it in two, in one bite," he said, and opened his monstrous jaws to show his six rows of teeth. "If I can make a mark in an anchor I guess I can bite a stem like that in two."

"There it is," cried the whale. "Look how it moves, twisting and turning." The whale thought he had better eyesight than the others. As a matter of fact he hadn't; what he had seen was merely an old conger eel, several yards long, that was swimming toward them.

"That fellow has never caused any commotion in the sea before, or frightened any other big fish," said the catfish with disgust. "I have met him often."

They told the conger about the new sea serpent and asked him if he wanted to go with them to discover what it was.

"I wonder if it is longer than I am," said the conger eel, and stretched himself. "If it is, then it will be sorry."

"It certainly will," said the rest of the company. "There are enough of us so we don't have to tolerate it if we don't want to!" they exclaimed, and hurried on.

They saw something that looked like a floating island that was having trouble keeping itself from sinking. It was an old whale. His head was overgrown with seaweed, and on his back were so many mussels and oysters that its black skin looked as if it had white spots.

"Come on, old man," the young whale said. "There is a new fish in the ocean and we won't tolerate it!"

"Oh, let me stay where I am!" grumbled the old whale. "Peace is all I ask, to be left in peace. Ow! Ow! . . . I am very sick, it will be the death of me. My only comfort is to let my back emerge above the water, then the sea gulls scratch it: the sweet birds. That helps a lot as long as they don't dig too deep with their bills and get into the blubber. There's the skeleton of one still sitting on my back. It got stuck and couldn't get loose when I had to submerge. The little fishes picked his bones clean. You can see it. . . . Look at him, and look at me. . . . Oh, I am very sick."

"You are just imagining all that," said the young whale. "I am not sick, no one that lives in the sea is ever sick."

"I am sorry!" said the old whale. "The eels have skin diseases, the carp have smallpox, and we all suffer from worms."

"Nonsense!" shouted the shark, who didn't like to listen to that kind of talk. Neither did the others, so they all swam on.

At last they came to the place where part of the telegraph cable lies, that stretches from Europe to America across sand shoals and high mountains, through endless forests of seaweed and coral. The currents move as the winds do in the heavens above, and through them swim schools of fishes, more numerous than the flocks of migratory birds that fly through the air. There was a noise, a sound, a humming, the ghost of which you hear in the great conch shell when you hold it up to your ear.

"There is the serpent!" shouted the bigger fish and the little fishes too. They had caught sight of some of the telegraph cable but neither the beginning nor the end of it, for they were both lost in the far distance. Sponges, polyps, and gorgonia swayed above it and leaned against it, sometimes hiding it from view. Sea urchins and snails climbed over it; and great crabs, like giant spiders, walked tightrope along it. Deep blue sea cucumbers—or whatever those

creatures are called who eat with their whole body—lay next to it; one would think that they were trying to smell it. Flounders and cod kept turning from side to side, in order to be able to listen to what everyone was saying. The starfishes had dug themselves down in the mire; only two of their points were sticking up, but they had eyes on them and were staring at the black snake, hoping to see something come out of it.

The telegraph cable lay perfectly still, as if it were lifeless; but inside, it was filled with life: with thoughts, human thoughts.

"That thing is treacherous," said the whale, "It might hit me in the stomach, and that is my weak point."

"Let's feel our way forward," said one of the polyps. "I have long arms and flexible fingers. I've already touched it, but now I'll take a firmer grasp."

And it stuck out its arms and encircled the cable. "I have felt both its stomach and its back. It is not scaly. I don't think it has any skin either. I don't believe it lays eggs and I don't think it gives birth to live children."

The conger eel lay down beside the cable and stretched itself as far as it could. "It is longer than I am," it admitted. "But length isn't everything. One has to have skin, a good stomach and, above all, suppleness."

The whale—the young strong whale!—bowed more deeply than it ever had before. "Are you a fish or a plant?" he asked. "Or are you a surface creation, one of those who can't live down here?"

The telegraph didn't answer, though it was filled with words. Thoughts traveled through it so fast that they took only seconds to move from one end to the other: hundreds of miles away.

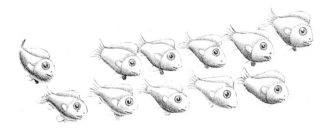

"Will you answer or be bitten in two?" asked the ill-mannered shark.

All the other fishes repeated the question: "Answer or be bitten in two?"

The telegraph cable didn't move; it had its own ideas, which isn't surprising for someone so full of thoughts. "Let them bite me in two," it thought. "Then I will be pulled up and repaired. It has happened to lots of my relations, that are not half as long as I am." But it didn't speak, it telegraphed; besides, it found the question impertinent; after all, it was lying there on official business.

Dusk had come. The sun was setting, as men say. It was firey red, and the clouds were as brilliant as fire—one more beautiful than the other.

"Now comes the red illumination," said the polyp. "Maybe the thing will be easier to see in that light, though I hardly think it worth looking at."

"Attack it! Attack it!" screamed the catfish, and showed all his teeth.

"Attack it! Attack it!" shouted the whale, the shark, the swordfish, and the conger eel.

They pushed forward. The catfish was first; but just as it was going to bite the cable the swordfish, who was a little too eager, stuck its sword into the behind of the cat fish. It was a mistake, but it kept the catfish from using the full strength of its jaw muscles.

There was a great muddle in the mud. The sea

cucumbers, the big fishes, and the small ones swam around in circles; they pushed and shoved and squashed and ate each other up. The crabs and the lobsters fought, and the snails pulled their heads into their houses. The telegraph cable just minded its own business, which is the proper thing for a telegraph cable to do.

Night came to the sky above, but down in the ocean millions and millions of little animals illuminated the water. Crayfish no larger than the head of a pin gave off light. It is incredible and wonderful; and quite true.

All the animals of the sea looked at the telegraph cable. "If only we knew what it was—or at least what it wasn't," said one of the fishes. And that was a very important question.

An old sea cow—human beings call them mermen and mermaids—came gliding by. This one was a mermaid. She had a tail and short arms for splashing, hanging breasts, and seaweed and parasites on her head—and of these she was very proud. "If you want learning and knowledge," she said, "then I think I am the best equipped to give it to you. But I want free passage on the bottom of the sea for myself and my family. I am a fish like you, and a reptile by training. I am the most intelligent citizen of the ocean. I know about everything under the water and everything above it. The thing that you are worrying about comes from up there; and everything from above is dead and powerless, once it comes down here. So let it lie, it is only a human invention and of no importance."

"I think it may be more than that," said the tiny fish.

"Shut up, mackerel!" said the sea cow.

"Shrimp!" shouted the others, and they meant it as an insult.

The sea cow explained to them that the sea serpent who had frightened them—the cable itself, by the way, didn't make a sound—was not dangerous. It was only an invention of those animals up on dry land called human beings. When she finished talking about the sea serpent, she gave a little lesson in the craftiness and wickedness of men: "They are always trying to catch us. That is the only reason for their existence. They throw down nets, traps and long fishing lines that have hooks, with bait attached to them, to try and fool us. This is probably another— bigger—fishing line. They are so stupid that they expect us to bite on it. But we aren't as dumb as that. Don't touch that piece of junk. It will unravel, fall apart, and become mud and mire—the whole thing. Let it lie there and rot. Anything that comes from above is worthless; it breaks or creaks; it is no good!"

"No good!" said all the creatures of the sea, accepting the mermaid's opinion in order to have one.

The little tiny fish didn't agree, but it had learned to keep its thoughts to itself. "That enormously long snake may be the most marvelous fish in the sea. I have a feeling that it is."

"Marvelous!" we human beings agree; and we can prove that it is true.

The great sea serpent of the fable has become a fact. It was constructed by human skill, conceived by human intelligence. It stretches from the Eastern Hemisphere to the Western, carrying messages from country to country faster than light travels from the sun down to the earth. Each year the great serpent grows. Soon it will stretch across all the great oceans, under the storm-whipped waves and the glasslike water, through which the skipper can look down as if he were sailing though the air and see the multitude of fish and the fireworks of color.

At the very depths is a *Midgards-worm,* biting its own tail as it circumscribes the world. Fish and reptiles hit their heads against it; it is impossible to understand what it is by looking at it. Human thoughts expressed in all the languages of the world, and yet silent: the snake of knowledge of good and evil. The most wonderful of the wonders of the sea: our time's great sea serpent!

ALL GONE
WALTER DE LA MARE

There was once a cat called Slyboots, who, after having lived most of her life with a rich widow in a very comfortable house, suddenly found herself without a home. She had seen a good deal of the world, and knew how hard it might prove for a creature like herself no longer young and in this sad state of affairs to live easy. Besides, she was indolent by nature, had been brought up in luxury, and could only hope for the best. With this in mind, she struck up an acquaintance with a mouse. At first they merely exchanged the time of day; and if they met by chance in one of the rooms of the empty mansion, it was the mouse who was quickly gone. And when, later, it came to a little talk and gossiping between them, the mouse much preferred to be on the other side of her hole in the wainscot. But she was a simple and good-natured little creature, if vain and fond of flattery, and was so proud of her fine new acquaintance that she at length put aside all doubts, qualms and misgivings, and agreed to keep house with the cat.

A very good bargain this was for Slyboots. The mouse had not only agreed to do all the housework—

sweep, dust, tidy and keep things neat and trim; but she it was who at night went scampering off in the dark from house to house, snuffing out wheresoever good food and dainties were to be found—meat and marrow, bones and scraps, cheese and butter. She knew every cranny and crevice and hole; and if any larder door had been left ajar, the cat soon heard of it. All Slyboots had to do was to steal out and fetch in what they needed (and the mouse needed very little), and to idle away the rest of the day in day-dreaming and drowsing at home in ease and idleness. It was a hot and thundery summer when first they met, no weather for exercise; so this way of life suited her very well; and she never ceased whispering sly pleasant little speeches in the mouse's small round ear whenever she appeared in sight or they sat together at meals. And so the time went by until it drew on towards autumn.

"There is one little matter that is troubling me," said the cat one evening, after a private look round the house when the mouse had been out marketing. "A trifle as yet, my dear, but yet worth your pondering over. We have *no* provision for the winter. Not a morsel. And, since we are now living alone, we have none of these clumsy, selfish humans to help us. Winter will be our hungry time. I am strong and lusty and can, of course, fend for myself. It's little you I am thinking of. It troubles me. The cold will come—frost and snow and bitter winds. Doors and windows will be shut. You musn't risk your precious life too often. There are traps, and I know what a temptation toasted cheese may be; there are—er—hungry enemies always in wait. Now what shall we do about the winter?"

At this, the simple mouse could scarcely contain her-self for pride. "Ah, my dear friend, I long ago thought of that. When I was living alone. Before I had your precious, precious company. Come with me, and you shall share a little secret."

Without another word she went into the back parts of a dusty old closet and showed the cat where, by hook and by crook, she had stowed away a fine, large, earthen-ware gallipot brim-full of fat. "That jar, my dear, contains all my hard-won savings; and I would rather starve than waste it."

"Starve," said the cat, and stared, her tail-tip twitch-ing softly from side to side. She sniffed. She purred. "Excellent," she cried again and again. "How clever! How ingenious! How thoughtful and how wise! There is but one little doubt in my mind, my dear. Is this cupboard safe? Surely the rats or—other creatures—might get in here *any* fine moonlight night."

At this the mouse was much alarmed. At length, after long and anxious discussion, the cat said, "Wainscots are good, cupboards are good, cellars are good; so are holes in the ground, hollows in trees, empty houses, caves, chasms and grottoes. But there is no place in the wide world, my dear, where a treasure like ours can be more safely stowed away than in a church. A church. Not even the wickedest thieves and robbers would dare to steal anything out of a church. St. Thomas's is the very place. It's cold. Most days it's empty, and there is a broken pane of glass under the belfry. I know the very place where we can hide the pot— behind a stone tomb, my dear—where no-one would look for it. It shall be done to-morrow; and we will not so much as touch, taste or even think of it until we are really and truly in *need* of it. No, my dear."

So towards evening next day they set out together to

the church. The pot was hidden in its niche behind the tomb, not a soul being by to see them there. And as darkness came on, they stole out of the church and returned home. The days passed in peace and quiet; and they seemed to be closer friends than ever.

But it was not very long before the cat began to grow a little weary of the mouse's company, looks and ways; and to pine on and on even for but just one secret sniff of the great gallipot of fat. As time went on she could think of little else; and, paws tucked in, would sit brooding all day in a corner, sulky and silent.

"I hope, dear friend," said the mouse at last, "you are not in any trouble, not indisposed, not ill?"

"Dear me, no!" the cat replied. "*Me*, ill! Never. Still, there is a little something on my mind. It is this. My favourite cousin who lives nine streets away has just brought a small, handsome son into the world. A beautiful little creature, creamy-white with cinnamon-brown patches, and I have been asked to be his godmother. They live in a fine house, and on the fat of the land; and it is, of course, a great honour. No need to tell *you* that, my dear! But I have been unable to decide whether or not to go to this christening only because I felt that, well, you *might* be a little hurt—a *little* hurt perhaps, at not having been asked to come too."

"Hurt!" said the mouse, stifling a gasp and a shiver at the very thought of being a guest in such a company. "Certainly not, my dear. I'll take every care of the house while you are gone, and shall be almost as happy alone thinking of you in the feasting and merrymaking as if I were with you. And if there *should* be any morsel very much to my taste at the christening, I am sure you will remember me. There's nothing like a sip and a suppet of sweet red christening wine! Please not to forget me!"

But the cat had no such cousin, not she. Nor had she been invited to be a godmother. By no means. Without another word, she slipped out of doors, and first this turning, then that, stole on and made her way straight to the church, looked, listened, then crawled in through the hole in the belfry window which was easily wide enough to admit her without brushing her whiskers. Once safe inside, in the cool great empty place, she had soon pushed off the lid of the pot. Crouched up in the niche behind the stone image, she at once set to at her feast.

Nor did she desist until she had licked off the complete upper layer of the rich ripe fat. After which, well fed, she replaced the pot in its hiding-place, stole out of the church, and took a walk upon the roofs of the town, on the lookout for other little opportunities. She then stretched herself out in the sun, sleeked herself with her long well-oiled tongue from chin to tail-tip, licking her chops whenever she thought of her feast; composed herself for a nap, and it was far on in the evening before she returned home.

"So here you are," said the mouse, "safe and sound. I've waited supper, my dear. But I was beginning to get anxious. I hope you've had a happy day."

"Happy enough," said the cat.

"And what name did they give the infant?"

"'Name?' 'Name?'" repeated the cat. "Why Top-off!"

"Topoff!" murmured the mouse. "*Topoff*! That is an odd, uncommon name—a very odd name."

"Usual or not, what does it signify?" said the cat. "It's no worse than *Crumbstealer* or *Cheesepicker*, I suppose, as so

many of *your* godchildren seem or ought to be called."
And at that the mouse fell silent.

Before long Mistress Slyboots was seized with yet
another fit of longing for the fat. The savour and sweetness
of the pot haunted her very dreams. And at last she said to
the mouse, "You must do me yet another favour, my dear,
and once more for an hour or two manage the house in my
absence. I am again asked to be godmother, friends at a
little distance too—and, as this time the infant is jet-black
with a milk-white ring round its neck, a rare thing indeed
if you knew anything about it, I simply cannot refuse."

The good kind mouse consented, and, waving
Slyboots farewell from the porch, returned humbly into

the house. And she—the cat—sly, gluttonous creature—
she crept out once more by her short cuts and along the
town walls to the church, and in at St. Thomas's window.
And this time she half emptied the delicious pot of fat.

"It's a strange thing," she thought to herself licking
her chops, now this side, now that, "but nothing in this
world ever tastes so good as the dainties one keeps to
oneself." And she was well satisfied with her day's work.

The stars were already shining bright by the time she
came back home. And a glossy, comfortable creature she
looked as she stepped delicately into the house.

"And what is the name of your god-child this time?"
enquired the mouse.

"'Name?' 'This time?' What a nose, my dear, you
have for trifles! Why Half-gone," answered the cat, with
an inward grin.

"*Halfgone*! do you say? Well! Halfgone! I never heard
so strange a name in the whole of my life! I'll wager *that*
name's not in the Calendar!"

"The Calendar," cried the cat, "what's the Calendar
to me? *Halfgone* was the name I said; and a plump, needle-
clawed, silky-whiskered little creature it is." The mouse
trembled a little at sight of her speaking these words, and
presently crept off to bed.

For a time matters went much as usual; and all was
friendly once more. But not so many days had gone by
before the cat's mouth began to water again. She would
actually wake up in the middle of the morning, licking her
chops at rich flavours which although they were but
memories seemed to be on her very tongue. She paced
about, restless and yawning, stared at nothing, and became
so contrary and morose that her house-mate the mouse

would hide herself away in her room for hours together merely to be out of reach of her sullen stare.

And then one fine October afternoon, the cat delayed no longer, but cried out in a loud voice to the mouse: "All good things go in threes, my dear. You will scarcely credit it; but I am asked to stand godmother yet again. This time the child is rarest tortoiseshell—of a pattern and colouring never seen outside a Queen's palace. It has opened its eyes, and it mews, my dear, a complete octave—an infant seven days old! Think of it! Why, it can happen but once in a century—if that. But it's blood that tells. I hate, I grieve, I can't endure to leave you lonely, beds unmade, rooms unswept. But how can I help myself? How can I resist? And you so much amused at my family names! Ah, well; I bear no grudge. Jeer if it pleases you. I shall not be hurt."

"*Top off! Halfgone!*" murmured the mouse. "They were certainly odd names. They made me a little thoughtful. Perhaps you are growing a little tired of me. And now another to come!"

"Ah, but you sit at home," said the cat, "in your demure dark-grey fur coat and that long dainty tail, and you are filled with fancies. That's because you so seldom venture out in the day-time. You are *too* dainty, you don't eat enough. No variety: nothing rich. You think too much. We must keep up with the times. We must turn over a new leaf." With that she pricked up her whiskers, and off she went.

During the cat's absence the mouse cleaned the house from top to bottom, putting everything in spotless trim. And while she scrubbed and polished, there was no time for sad, perplexing thoughts.

Meanwhile Slyboots was cowering greedily over the pot in the church; and this time she licked it as clean as a whistle. There wasn't a speck, not a vestige or flavour of fat left.

"When everything is finished, one may have a little peace," she said to herself. And thoroughly satisfied, she enjoyed a long dreamless sleep in the sunshine, took a jaunt through the town, gossiped with friends, saw the sights, and did not return home till well after midnight. At the first whisper of her at the door, the mouse looked out and at once enquired what name had been chosen for the third child.

"It will give you no more pleasure than the others," said the cat, with a surly glare. "We called him *All-gone*."

"*'Allgone!'*" cried the mouse. "*'Allgone!'* Oh, but how strange, how outlandish a name! Never in all my born days could I believe there was such a name. *Allgone!* Never. Nowhere."

"Well," said the cat, "you have heard it now. And that's the end of that." Whereupon she yawned as if her head would split in two, and went off to bed.

From that night on, Slyboots received no further invitation to stand godmother, and was so short with the mouse when she enquired after her three godchildren that little more was said about the matter. Summer gone, she grew more and more sulky and ill-natured as the days of autumn drew in, and hardly ceased complaining of the food, professing that she was an invalid, had a dainty stomach and needed constant care and every nourishment.

At last, one cold frosty morning the mouse crept up to her bedside and said, "My dear, it is nearly winter now. There is scarcely anything but rinds of vegetables to be

found outside. Do you not agree it would be a very pleasant thing if we started off together and enjoyed just a taste
or two of our pot of fat?"

Her face twinkled all over at the thought of it; and
indeed, poor thing, having been so long skimped even of
her crumbs, she was by now little but a packet of bones.

The cat opened her mouth as she lay in bed: "By all
means," said she, "by all means. And you will enjoy your
taste as you call it exactly as much as you would enjoy
putting out that dainty tongue of yours at the window to
flout the full moon!"

"What can *that* mean?" thought the mouse to
herself. But she was too much excited to put her question into words. Off she scampered to make ready for
the journey.

They set out, and as soon as the sexton's back was
turned among the gravestones, they crept in at the belfry
window. So cold and stony and gloomy was it inside the
great church that a shiver ran down the mouse's spine,
while her mouth watered the more. And at last they came
to the hiding-place. And there was the pot, its parchment
top tied down, and as neat as a new pin

And the cat said, grinning, "My dear, *you* shall open
it; *you* shall have first nibble; *you* shall first enjoy what we
have so long been looking forward to. But leave a morsel
for me!"

Whereupon Mistress Mouse nibbled through the
string, pushed off the cover, paused and stared. The pot
was empty. Bare.

"Oh! Ah! Alas! Alackaday!" broke out Slyboots in a
wild shrill caterwauling. "Robbers, robbers! Thieves,
thieves!" Her voice echoed dreadful and hollow in the cold

church, and died away. The mouse turned slowly, and out of her little round bright jet-black eyes gazed at her friend.

"Aha!" she cried bitterly, "I see; oh, I see. Now I begin to understand. Now I know. Friend that you professed yourself; true, faithful friend that you *are*! First it was '*Topoff*'. Next it was '*Halfgone*'. And last it was . . . ."

"Hold your tongue this instant," yelled the cat, bristling all over. "Another syllable, and—"

" '*Allgone*,'" squeaked the mouse with her last breath.

For scarcely were the words out of her mouth, when Slyboots, claws extended, and with a yell of rage, had pounced upon her and swallowed her down.

"Truly," said she, as she turned away from the empty pot, and sallied out of the church, "that was a sad end to an old friendship. But such is the way of the world."

THE BEGINNING OF THE ARMADILLOES

RUDYARD KIPLING

This, O Best Beloved, is another story of the High and Far-Off Times. In the very middle of those times was a Stickly-Prickly Hedgehog, and he lived on the banks of the turbid Amazon, eating shelly snails and things. And he had a friend, a Slow-Solid Tortoise, who lived on the banks of the turbid Amazon, eating green lettuces and things. And so *that* was all right, Best Beloved. Do you see?

But also, and at the same time, in those High and Far-Off Times, there was a Painted Jaguar, and he lived on the banks of the turbid Amazon too; and he ate everything that he could catch. When he could not catch deer or monkeys he would eat frogs and beetles; and when he could not catch frogs and beetles he went to his Mother Jaguar, and she told him how to eat hedgehogs and tortoises.

She said to him ever so many times, graciously waving her tail, "My son, when you find a Hedgehog you must drop him into the water and then he will uncoil, and when you catch a Tortoise you must scoop him out of his shell with your paw." And so that was all right, Best Beloved.

One beautiful night on the banks of the turbid Amazon, Painted Jaguar found Stickly-Prickly Hedgehog and Slow-and-Solid Tortoise sitting under the trunk of a fallen tree. They could not run away, and so Stickly-Prickly curled himself up into a ball, because he was a Hedgehog, and Slow-and-Solid Tortoise drew in his head and feet into his shell as far as they would go, because he was a Tortoise; and so that was all right, Best Beloved. Do you see?

"Now attend to me," said Painted Jaguar, "because this is very important. My mother said that when I meet a Hedgehog I am to drop him into the water and then he will uncoil, and when I meet a Tortoise I am to scoop him out of his shell with my paw. Now which of you is Hedgehog and which is Tortoise? because, to save my spots, I can't tell."

"Are you sure of what your Mummy told you?" said Stickly-Prickly Hedgehog. "Are you quite sure? Perhaps she said that when you uncoil a Tortoise you must shell him out of the water with a scoop, and when you paw a Hedgehog you must drop him on the shell."

"Are you sure of what your Mummy told you? said Slow-and-Solid Tortoise. "Are you quite sure? Perhaps she said that when you water a Hedgehog you must drop him into your paw, and when you meet a Tortoise you must shell him till he uncoils."

"I don't think it was at all like that," said Painted Jaguar, but he felt a little puzzled; "but, please, say it again more distinctly."

"When you scoop water with your paw you uncoil it with a Hedgehog," said Stickly-Prickly. "Remember that, because it's important."

"*But*," said the Tortoise, "when you paw your meat you drop it into a Tortoise with a scoop. Why can't you understand?"

"You are making my spots ache," said Painted Jaguar; "and besides, I didn't want your advice at all. I only wanted to know which of you is Hedgehog and which is Tortoise."

"I shan't tell you," said Stickly-Prickly. But you can scoop me out of my shell if you like."

"Aha!" said Painted Jaguar. "Now I know you're Tortoise. You thought I wouldn't! Now I will." Painted Jaguar darted out his paddy-paw just as Stickly-Prickly curled himself up, and of course Jaguar's paddy-paw was just filled with prickles. Worse than that, he knocked Stickly-Prickly away and away into the woods and the bushes, where it was too dark to find him. Then he put his paddy-paw into his mouth, and of course the prickles hurt him worse than ever. As soon as he could speak he said, "Now I know he isn't Tortoise at all. But'—and then he scratched his head with his un-prickly paw—'how do I know that this other is Tortoise?"

"But I *am* Tortoise," said Slow-and-Solid. "Your mother was quite right. She said that you were to scoop me out of my shell with your paw. Begin."

"You didn't say she said that a minute ago," said Painted Jaguar, sucking the prickles out of his paddy-paw. 'You said she said something quite different."

"Well, suppose you say that I said that she said something quite different, I don't see that it makes any difference; because if she said what you said I said she said, it's just the same as if I said what she said she said. On the other hand, if you think she said that you were to uncoil me with a scoop, instead of pawing me into drops with a shell, I can't help that, can I?"

"But you said you wanted to be scooped out of your shell with my paw," said Painted Jaguar.

"If you'll think again you'll find that I didn't say anything of the kind. I said that your mother said that you were to scoop me out of my shell," said Slow-and-Solid.

"What will happen if I do?" said the Jaguar most sniffily and most cautious.

"I don't know, because I've never been scooped out of my shell before; but I tell you truly, if you want to see me swim away you've only got to drop me into the water."

"I don't believe it," said Painted Jaguar. "You've mixed up all the things my mother told me to do with the things that you asked me whether I was sure that she didn't say, till I don't know whether I'm on my head or my painted tail; and now you come and tell me something I *can* understand, and it makes me more mixy than before. My mother told me that I was to drop one of you two into the water, and as you seem so anxious to be dropped I think you don't want to be dropped. So jump into the turbid Amazon and be quick about it."

"I warn you that your Mummy won't be pleased. Don't tell her I didn't tell you," said Slow-and-Solid.

"If you say another word about what my mother said—' the Jaguar answered, but he had not finished the sentence before Slow-and-Solid quietly dived into the turbid Amazon, swam under water for a long way, and came out on the bank where Stickly-Prickly was waiting for him.

"That was a very narrow escape," said Stickly-Prickly. "I don't like Painted Jaguar. What did you tell him that you were?"

"I told him truthfully that I was a truthful Tortoise, but he wouldn't believe it, and he made me jump into the river to see if I was, and I was, and he is surprised. Now he's gone to tell his Mummy. Listen to him!"

They could hear Painted Jaguar roaring up and down among the trees and the bushes by the side of the turbid Amazon, till his Mummy came.

"Son, son!" said his mother ever so many times, graciously waving her tail, "what have you been doing that you shouldn't have done?"

"I tried to scoop something that said it wanted to be scooped out of its shell with my paw, and my paw is full of per-ickles," said Painted Jaguar.

"Son, son!" said his mother ever so many times,

graciously waving her tail, "by the prickles in your paddy-paw I see that that must have been a Hedgehog. You should have dropped him into the water."

"I did that to the other thing; and he said he was a Tortoise, and I didn't believe him, and it was quite true, and he has dived under the turbid Amazon, and he won't come up again, and I haven't anything at all to eat, and I think we had better find lodgings somewhere else. They are too clever on the turbid Amazon for poor me!"

"Son, son!" said his mother ever so many times, graciously waving her tail, "now attend to me and remember what I say. A Hedgehog curls himself up into a ball and his prickles stick out every which way at once. By this you may know the Hedgehog."

"I don't like this old lady one little bit," said Stickly-Prickly, under the shadow of a large leaf. "I wonder what else she knows?"

"A Tortoise can't curl himself up," Mother Jaguar went on, ever so many times, graciously waving her tail. "He only draws his head and legs into his shell. By this you may know the Tortoise."

"I don't like this old lady at all—at all," said Slow-and-Solid Tortoise. "Even Painted Jaguar can't forget those directions. It's a great pity that you can't swim, Stickly-Prickly."

"Don't talk to me," said Stickly-Prickly. "Just think how much better it would be if you could curl up. This *is* a mess! Listen to Painted Jaguar."

Painted Jaguar was sitting on the banks of the turbid Amazon sucking prickles out of his paw and saying to himself—

"Can't curl, but can swim—
Slow-Solid, that's him!
Curls up, but can't swim—
Stickly-Prickly, that's him!"

"He'll never forget that this month of Sundays," said Stickly-Prickly. "Hold up my chin, Slow-and-Solid. I'm going to try to learn to swim. It may be useful."

"Excellent!" said Slow-and-Solid; and he held up Stickly-Prickly's chin, while Stickly-Prickly kicked in the waters of the turbid Amazon.

"You'll make a fine swimmer yet," said Slow-and-Solid. "Now, if you can unlace my backplates a little, I'll see what I can do towards curling up. It may be useful."

Stickly-Prickly helped to unlace Tortoise's back-plates, so that by twisting and straining Slow-and-Solid actually managed to curl up a tiddy wee bit.

"Excellent!" said Stickly-Prickly; "but I shouldn't do any more just now. It's making you black in the face. Kindly lead me into the water once again and I'll practise that side-stroke which you say is so easy." And so Stickly-Prickly practised, and Slow-and-Solid swam alongside.

"Excellent!" said Slow-and-Solid. "A little more practice will make you a regular whale. Now, if I may trouble you to unlace my back and front plates two holes more, I'll try that fascinating bend that you say is so easy. Won't Painted Jaguar be surprised!"

"Excellent!" said Stickly-Prickly, all wet from the turbid Amazon. "I declare, I shouldn't know you from one of my own family. Two holes, I think, you said? A little more expression, please, and don't grunt quite so

much, or Painted Jaguar may hear us. When you've finished, I want to try that long dive which you say is so easy.
Won't Painted Jaguar be surprised!"

And so Stickly-Prickly dived, and Slow-and-Solid
dived alongside.

"Excellent!" said Slow-and-Solid. "A leetle more
attention to holding your breath and you will be able to
keep house at the bottom of the turbid Amazon. Now I'll
try that exercise of wrapping my hind legs round my ears
which you say is so peculiarly comfortable. Won't Painted
Jaguar be surprised!"

"Excellent!" said Stickly-Prickly. "But it's straining
your backplates a little. They are all overlapping now,
instead of lying side by side."

"Oh, that's the result of exercise," said Slow-and-
Solid. "I've noticed that your prickles seem to be melting
into one another, and that you're growing to look rather
more like a pine-cone, and less like a chestnut-burr, than
you used to."

"Am I?" said Stickly-Prickly. "That comes from my
soaking in the water. Oh, won't Painted Jaguar be
surprised!"

They went on with their exercises, each helping the
other, till morning came; and when the sun was high they
rested and dried themselves. Then they saw that they were
both of them quite different from what they had been.

"Stickly-Prickly," said Tortoise after breakfast, "I am
not what I was yesterday; but I think that I may yet amuse
Painted Jaguar."

"That was the very thing I was thinking just now,"
said Stickly-Prickly. "I think scales are a tremendous
improvement on prickles—to say nothing of being able to

swim. Oh, *won't* Painted Jaguar be surprised! Let's go and find him."

By and by they found Painted Jaguar, still nursing his paddy-paw that had been hurt the night before. He was so astonished that he fell three times backward over his own painted tail without stopping.

"Good morning!" said Stickly-Prickly. "And how is your dear gracious Mummy this morning?"

"She is quite well, thank you," said Painted Jaguar, "but you must forgive me if I do not at this precise moment recall your name."

"That's unkind of you," said Stickly-Prickly, "seeing that this time yesterday you tried to scoop me out of my shell with your paw."

"But you hadn't any shell. It was all prickles," said Painted Jaguar. "I know it was. Just look at my paw!"

"You told me to drop into the turbid Amazon and be drowned," said Slow-and-Solid. "Why are you so rude and forgetful today?"

"Don't you remember what your mother told you?" said Stickly-Prickly,—

> "Can't curl, but can swim—
> Stickly-Prickly, that's him!
> Curls up, but can't swim—
> Slow-Solid, that's him!"

Then they both curled themselves up and rolled round and round Painted Jaguar till his eyes turned truly cart-wheels in his head.

Then he went to fetch his mother.

"Mother," he said, "there are two new animals in the woods today, and the one that you said couldn't swim, swims, and the one that you said couldn't curl up, curls; and they've gone shares in their prickles, I think, because both of them are scaly all over, instead of one being smooth and the other very prickly; and, besides that, they are rolling round and round in circles, and I don't feel comfy."

"Son, son!" said Mother Jaguar ever so many times, graciously waving her tail, "a Hedgehog is a Hedgehog, and can't be anything but a Hedgehog; and a Tortoise is a Tortoise, and can never be anything else."

"But it isn't a Hedgehog, and it isn't a Tortoise. It's a little bit of both, and I don't know its proper name."

"Nonsense!" said Mother Jaguar. "Everything has its proper name. I should call it Armadillo till I found out the real one. And I should leave it alone."

So Painted Jaguar did as he was told, especially about leaving them alone; but the curious thing is that from that day to this, O Best Beloved, no one on the banks of the turbid Amazon has ever called Stickly-Prickly and Slow-and-Solid anything except Armadillo. There are Hedgehogs and Tortoises in other places, of course (there are some in my garden); but the real old and clever kind, with their scales lying lippety-lappety one over the other, like pine-cone scales, that lived on the banks of the turbid Amazon in the High and Far-Off Days, are always called Armadilloes, because they were so clever.

So *that's* all right, Best Beloved. Do you see?

> I've never sailed the Amazon,
> > I've never reached Brazil;
> But the *Don* and the *Magdalena*,
> > They can go there when they will!

Yes, weekly from Southampton,
Great Steamers, white and gold,
Go rolling down to Rio
(Roll down—roll down to Rio!)
And I'd like to roll to Rio
Some day before I'm old!

I've never seen a Jaguar,
Nor yet an Armadill—
O dilloing in his armour,
And I s'pose I never will,

Unless I go to Rio
These wonders to behold—
Roll down—roll down to Rio—
Roll really down to Rio!
Oh, I'd love to roll to Rio
Some day before I'm old!

THE MONKEY AND THE JELLY-FISH

A Japanese Fairytale

ANDREW LANG

Children must often have wondered why jelly-fishes have no shells, like so many of the creatures that are washed up every day on the beach. In old times this was not so; the jelly-fish had as hard a shell as any of them, but he lost it through his own fault, as may be seen in this story.

The sea-queen Otohime, whom you read of in the story of Uraschimatoro, grew suddenly very ill. The swiftest messengers were sent hurrying to fetch the best doctors from every country under the sea, but it was all of no use; the queen grew rapidly worse instead of better. Everyone had almost given up hope, when one day a doctor arrived who was cleverer than the rest, and said that the only thing that would cure her was the liver of an ape. Now apes do not dwell under the sea, so a council of the wisest heads in the nation was called to consider the question how a liver could be obtained. At length it was decided that the turtle, whose prudence was well known, should swim to land and contrive to catch a living ape and bring him safely to the ocean kingdom.

It was easy enough for the council to entrust this mission to the turtle, but not at all so easy for him to fulfil it. However he swam to a part of the coast that was covered with tall trees, where he thought the apes were likely to be; for he was old, and had seen many things. It was some time before he caught sight of any monkeys, and he often grew tired with watching for them, so that one hot day he fell fast asleep, in spite of all his efforts to keep awake. By-and-by some apes, who had been peeping at him from the tops of the trees, where they had been carefully hidden from the turtle's eyes, stole noiselessly down, and stood round staring at him, for they had never seen a turtle before, and did not know what to make of it. At last one young monkey, bolder than the rest, stooped down and stroked the shining shell that the strange new creature wore on its back. The movement, gentle though it was, woke the turtle. With one sweep he seized the monkey's hand in his mouth, and held it tight, in spite of every effort to pull it away. The other apes, seeing that the turtle was not to be trifled with, ran off, leaving their young brother to his fate.

Then the turtle said to the monkey, 'If you will be quiet, and do what I tell you, I won't hurt you. But you must get on my back and come with me.'

The monkey, seeing there was no help for it, did as he was bid; indeed he could not have resisted, as his hand was still in the turtle's mouth.

Delighted at having secured his prize, the turtle hastened back to the shore and plunged quickly into the water. He swam faster than he had ever done before, and soon reached the royal palace. Shouts of joy broke forth from the attendants when he was seen approaching, and some of them ran to tell the queen that the monkey was there, and that before long she would be as well as ever she was. In fact, so great was their relief that they gave the monkey such a kind welcome, and were so anxious to make him happy and comfortable, that he soon forgot all the fears that had beset him as to his fate, and was generally quite at his ease, though every now and then a fit of home-sickness would come over him, and he would hide himself in some dark corner till it had passed away.

It was during one of these attacks of sadness that a jelly-fish happened to swim by. At that time jelly-fishes had shells. At the sight of the gay and lively monkey crouching under a tall rock, with his eyes closed and his head bent, the jelly-fish was filled with pity, and stopped, saying, 'Ah, poor fellow, no wonder you weep; a few days more, and they will come and kill you and give your liver to the queen to eat.'

The monkey shrank back horrified at these words and asked the jelly-fish what crime he had committed that deserved death.

'Oh, none at all,' replied the jelly-fish, 'but your liver is the only thing that will cure our queen, and how can we get at it without killing you? You had better submit to your fate, and make no noise about it, for though I pity you from my heart there is no way of helping you.' Then he went away, leaving the ape cold with horror.

At first he felt as if his liver was already being taken from his body, but soon he began to wonder if there was no means of escaping this terrible death, and at length he invented a plan which he thought would do. For a few days he pretended to be gay and happy as before, but when the sun went in, and rain fell in torrents, he wept and howled from dawn to dark, till the turtle, who was his head keeper, heard him, and came to see what was the

matter. Then the monkey told him that before he left home he had hung his liver out on a bush to dry, and if it was always going to rain like this it would become quite useless. And the rogue made such a fuss and moaning that he would have melted a heart of stone, and nothing would content him but that somebody should carry him back to land and let him fetch his liver again.

The queen's councillors were not the wisest of people, and they decided between them that the turtle should take the monkey back to his native land and allow him to get his liver off the bush, but desired the turtle not to lose sight of his charge for a single moment. The monkey knew this, but trusted to his power of beguiling the turtle when the time came, and mounted on his back with feelings of joy, which he was, however, careful to conceal. They set out, and in a few hours were wandering about the forest where the ape had first been caught, and when the monkey saw his family peering out from the tree tops, he swung himself up by the nearest branch, just managing to save his hind leg from being seized by the turtle. He told them all the dreadful things that had happened to him, and gave a war cry which brought the rest of the tribe from the neighbouring hills. At a word from him they rushed in a body to the unfortunate turtle, threw him on his back, and tore off the shield that covered his body. Then with mocking words they hunted him to the shore, and into the sea, which he was only too thankful to reach alive. Faint and exhausted he entered the queen's palace, for the cold of the water struck upon his naked body, and made him feel ill and miserable. But wretched though he was, he had to appear before the queen's advisers and tell them all that had befallen him, and how he had suffered the monkey to escape. But, as sometimes happens, the turtle was allowed to go scot-free, and had his shell given back to him, and all the punishment fell on the poor jelly-fish, who was condemned by the queen to go shieldless for ever after.

THE LAST OF THE DRAGONS

E. NESBITT

Of course you know that dragons were once as common as motor-omnibuses are now, and almost as dangerous. But as every well-brought-up prince was expected to kill a dragon, and rescue a princess, the dragons grew fewer and fewer till it was often quite hard for a princess to find a dragon to be rescued from. And at last there were no more dragons in France and no more dragons in Germany, or Spain, or Italy, or Russia. There were some left in China, and are still, but they are cold and bronzy, and there were never any, of course, in America. But the last real live dragon left was in England, and of course that was a very long time ago, before what you call English History began. This dragon lived in Cornwall in the big caves amidst the rocks, and a very fine big dragon it was, quite seventy feet long from the tip of its fearful snout to the end of its terrible tail. It breathed fire and smoke, and rattled when it walked, because its scales were made of iron. Its wings were like half-umbrellas—or like bat's wings, only several thousand times bigger. Everyone was very frightened of it, and well they might be.

Now the King of Cornwall had one daughter, and

when she was sixteen, of course she would have to go and face the dragon: such tales are always told in royal nurseries at twilight, so the Princess knew what she had to expect. The dragon would not eat her, of course—because the prince would come and rescue her. But the Princess could not help thinking it would be much pleasanter to have nothing to do with the dragon at all—not even to be rescued from him. "All the princes I know are such very silly little boys," she told her father. "Why must I be rescued by a prince?"

"It's always done, my dear," said the King, taking his crown off and putting it on the grass, for they were alone in the garden, and even kings must unbend sometimes.

"Father, darling," said the Princess presently, when she had made a daisy chain and put it on the King's head, where the crown ought to have been. "Father, darling, couldn't we tie up one of the silly little princes for the dragon to look at—and then *I* could go and kill the dragon and rescue the prince? I fence much better than any of the princes we know."

"What an unladylike idea!" said the King, and put his crown on again, for he saw the Prime Minister coming with a basket of new-laid Bills for him to sign. "Dismiss the thought, my child. I rescued your mother from a dragon, and you don't want to set yourself up above her, I should hope?"

"But this is the *last* dragon. It is different from all other dragons."

"How?" asked the King.

"Because he *is* the last," said the Princess, and went off to her fencing lessons, with which she took great pains. She took great pains with all her lessons—for she could

not give up the idea of fighting the dragon. She took such pains that she became the strongest and boldest and most skilful and most sensible princess in Europe. She had always been the prettiest and nicest.

And the days and years went on, till at last the day came which was the day before the Princess was to be rescued from the dragon. The Prince who was to do this deed of valour was a pale prince, with large eyes and a head full of mathematics and philosophy, but he had unfortunately neglected his fencing lessons. He was to stay the night at the palace, and there was a banquet.

After supper the Princess sent her pet parrot to the Prince with a note. it said:

"Please, Prince, come on to the terrace. I want to talk

to you without anybody else hearing.—The Princess."

So, of course, he went—and he saw her gown of silver a long way off shining among the shadows of the trees like water in starlight. And when he came quite close to her he said: "Princess, at your service," and bent his cloth-of-gold-covered knee and put his hand on his cloth-of-gold-covered heart.

"Do you think," said the Princess earnestly, "that you will be able to kill the dragon?"

"I will kill the dragon," said the Prince firmly, "or perish in the attempt."

"It's no use your perishing," said the Princess.

"It's the least I can do," said the Prince.

"What I'm afraid of is that it'll be the most you can do," said the Princess.

"It's the only thing I can do," said he, "unless I kill the dragon."

"Why you should do anything for me is what I can't see," said she.

"But I want to," he said. "You must know that I love you better than anything in the world."

When he said that he looked so kind that the Princess began to like him a little.

"Look here," she said, "no one else will go out tomorrow. You know they tie me to a rock and leave me—and then everybody scurries home and puts up the shutters and keeps them shut till you ride through the town in triumph shouting that you've killed the dragon, and I ride on the horse behind you weeping for joy."

"I've heard that that is how it is done," said he.

"Well, do you love me well enough to come very

quickly and set me free—and we'll fight the dragon together?"

"It wouldn't be safe for you."

"Much safer for both of us for me to be free, with a sword in my hand, than tied up and helpless. *Do* agree."

He could refuse her nothing. So he agreed. And next day everything happened as she had said.

When he had cut the cords that tied her to the rock they stood on the lonely mountain-side looking at each other.

"It seems to me," said the Prince, "that this ceremony could have been arranged without the dragon."

"Yes," said the Princess, "but since it has been arranged with the dragon—"

"It seems such a pity to kill the dragon—the last in the world," said the Prince.

"Well then, don't let's," said the Princess; "let's tame it not to eat princesses but to eat out of their hands. They say everything can be tamed by kindness."

"Taming by kindness means giving them things to eat," said the Prince. "Have you got anything to eat?"

She hadn't, but the Prince owned that he had a few biscuits. "Breakfast was so very early," said he, "and I thought you might have felt faint after the fight."

"How clever," said the Princess, and they took a biscuit in each hand. And they looked here, and they looked there, but never a dragon could they see.

"But here's its trail," said the Prince, and pointed to where the rock was scarred and scratched so as to make a track leading to a dark cave. It was like cart-ruts in a Sussex road, mixed with the marks of sea-gulls' feet on the sea-sand. "Look, that's where it's dragged its brass tail and planted its steel claws."

"Don't let's think how hard its tail and its claws are," said the Princess, "or I shall begin to be frightened—and I know you can't tame anything, even by kindness, if you're frightened of it. Come on. Now or never."

She caught the Prince's hand in hers and they ran along the path towards the dark mouth of the cave. But they did not run into it. It really was so very *dark*.

So they stood outside, and the Prince shouted: "What ho! Dragon there! What ho within!" And from the cave they heard an answering voice and great clattering and creaking. It sounded as though a rather large cotton-mill were stretching itself and waking up out of its sleep.

The Prince and the Princess trembled, but they stood firm.

"Dragon—I say, dragon!" said the Princess, "do come out and talk to us. We've brought you a present.

"Oh yes—I know your presents," growled the dragon in a huge rumbling voice. "One of those precious princesses, I suppose? And I've got to come out and fight for her. Well, I tell you straight, I'm not going to do it. A fair fight I wouldn't say no to—a fair fight and no favour—but one of these put-up fights where you've got to lose—no! So I tell you. If I wanted a princess I'd come and take her, in my own time—but I don't. What do you suppose I'd do with her, if I'd got her?"

"Eat her, wouldn't you?" said the Princess, in a voice that trembled a little.

"Eat a fiddle-stick end," said the dragon very rudely. "I wouldn't touch the horrid thing."

The Princess's voice grew firmer. "Do you like biscuits?" she said.

"No," growled the dragon.

"Not the nice little expensive ones with sugar on the top?"

"*No*," growled the dragon.

"Then what *do* you like?" asked the Prince.

"You go away and don't bother me," growled the dragon, and they could hear it turn over, and the clang and clatter of its turning echoed in the cave like the sound of the steam-hammers in the Arsenal at Woolwich.

The Prince and Princess looked at each other. What *were* they to do? Of course it was no use going home and telling the King that the dragon didn't want princesses—

because His Majesty was very old-fashioned and would never have believed that a new-fashioned dragon could ever be at all different from an old-fashioned dragon. They could not go into the cave and kill the dragon. Indeed, unless he attacked the Princess it did not seem fair to kill him at all.

"He must like something," whispered the Princess, and she called out in a voice as sweet as honey and sugar-cane:

"Dragon! Dragon dear!"

"WHAT?" shouted the dragon. "Say that again!" and they could hear the dragon coming towards them through the darkness of the cave. The Princess shivered, and said in a very small voice:

"Dragon! Dragon dear!"

And then the dragon came out. The Prince drew his sword, and the Princess drew hers—the beautiful silver-handled one that the Prince had brought in his motor-car. But they did not attack; they moved slowly back as the dragon came out, all the vast scaly length of him, and lay along the rock—his great wings half-spread and his silvery sheen gleaming like diamonds in the sun. At last they could retreat no further—the dark rock behind them stopped their way—and with their backs to the rock they stood swords in hand and waited.

The dragon drew nearer and nearer—and now they could see that he was not breathing fire and smoke as they had expected—he came crawling slowly towards them wriggling a little as a puppy does when it wants to play and isn't quite sure whether you're not cross with it.

And then they saw that great tears were coursing down its brazen cheek.

"Whatever's the matter?" said the Prince.

"Nobody," sobbed the dragon, "ever called me 'dear' before!"

"Don't cry, dragon dear," said the Princess. "We'll call you 'dear' as often as you like. We want to tame you."

"I *am* tame," said the dragon—"that's just it. That's what nobody but you has ever found out. I'm so tame that I'd eat out of your hands."

"Eat what, dragon dear?" said the Princess. "Not biscuits?" The dragon slowly shook his heavy head.

"Not biscuits?" said the Princess tenderly. "What, then, dragon dear?"

"Your kindness quite undragons me," it said. "No one has ever asked any of us what we like to eat—always offering us princesses, and then rescuing them—and never once, 'What'll you take to drink the King's health in?' Cruel hard I call it," and it wept again.

"But what would you like to drink our health in?" said the Prince. "We're going to be married today, aren't we, Princess?"

She said that she supposed so.

"What'll I take to drink your health in?" asked the dragon. "Ah, you're something like a gentleman, you are, sir. I don't mind if I do, sir. I'll be proud to drink your and your good lady's health in a tiny drop of"—its voice faltered—"to think of you asking me so friendly like," it said. "Yes, sir, just a tiny drop of puppuppuppuppupetrol—tha-that's what does a dragon good, sir—"

"I've lots in the car," said the Prince, and was off down the mountain like a flash. He was a good judge of character and he knew that with this dragon the Princess would be safe.

"If I might make so bold," said the dragon, "while the gentleman's away—p'raps just to pass the time you'd be so kind as to call me Dear again, and if you'd shake claws with a poor old dragon that's never been anybody's enemy but his own—well, the last of the dragons'll be the proudest dragon that's ever been since the first of them."

It held out an enormous paw, and the great steel hooks that were its claws closed over the Princess's hand as softly as the claws of the Himalayan bear will close over the bit of bun you hand it through the bars at the Zoo.

And so the Prince and Princess went back to the palace in triumph, the dragon following them like a pet dog. And all through the wedding festivities no one drank more earnestly to the happiness of the bride and bride-groom than the Princess's pet dragon—whom she had at once named Fido.

And when the happy pair were settled in their own kingdom, Fido came to them and begged to be allowed to make himself useful.

"There must be some little thing I can do," he said, rattling his wings and stretching his claws. "My wings and claws and so on ought to be turned to some account—to say nothing of my grateful heart."

So the Prince had a special saddle or howdah made for him—very long it was—like the tops of many tramcars fitted together. One hundred and fifty seats were fitted to this, and the dragon, whose greatest pleasure was now to give pleasure to others, delighted in taking parties of children to the seaside. It flew through the air quite easily with its hundred and fifty little passengers—and would lie on the sand patiently waiting till they were ready to return.

The children were very fond of it, and used to call it Dear, a word which never failed to bring tears of affection and gratitude to its eyes. So it lived, useful and respected, till quite the other day when someone happened to say, in his hearing, that dragons were out-of-date, now so much new machinery had come in. This so distressed him that he asked the King to change him into something less old-fashioned, and the kindly monarch at once changed him into a mechanical contrivance. The dragon, indeed, became the first aeroplane.

BABE, THE BLUE OX

Everyone knows and loves the legends of Paul Bunyan and his beloved ox, Babe. Paul was a lumberjack of the Maine woods in the olden days. He was so tall his cap touched the clouds and his legs were as big as the biggest trees. The legends tell of his amazing feats of strength, but he himself would always say he couldn't have done any of them without Babe.

ESTHER SHEPARD

Paul Bunyan couldn't of done all the great loggin' he did if it hadn't been for Babe the Blue Ox. I believe I mentioned helpin' to take care of him for a couple of months when I first come to camp, and then I helped measure him once afterwards for a new yoke Ole had to make for him. He'd broke the one he had when Paul was doin' an extra quick job haulin' lumber for some millmen down in Muskegon one summer, and Ole had to make him a new one right away and so we had to take Babe's measurements.

I've forgot most of the other figgurs, but I remember he measured forty-two axhandles between the eyes—and a tobacco box—you could easy fit in a Star tobacco box after the last axhandle. That tobacco box was lost and we couldn't never take the measurements again, but I remember that's what it was. And he weighed accordin'. Though he never was weighed that I know of, for there never was any scales made that would of been big enough.

Paul told Ole he might as well make him a new log chain too while he was at it—they generally never lasted no more'n about two months anyway, the way Babe pulled on 'em—and so we measured him up for the chain too. It generally took about four carloads of iron every time he had to have a new one.

Babe was so long in the body, Paul used to have to carry a pair of field-glasses around with him so as he could see what he was doin' with his hind feet.

One time Babe kicked one of the straw bosses in the head, so his brains all run out, but the cook happened to be handy and he filled the hole up with hotcake batter and plastered it together again and he was just as good as ever. And right now, if I'm not mistaken, that boss is runnin' camp for the Bigham Loggin' Company of Virginia, Minnesota.

Babe was so big that every time they shod him they had to open up a new iron mine on Lake Superior, and one time when Ole the Blacksmith carried one of his shoes a mile and a half he sunk a foot and half in solid rock at every step.

His color was blue—a fine, pretty, deep blue—and that's why he was called the Blue Ox—when you looked up at him the air even looked blue all around him. His nose was pretty near all black, but red on the inside, of course, and he had big white horns, curly on the upper section—about the upper third—and kind of darkish brown at the tip, and then the rest of him was all that same deep blue.

He didn't use to be always that blue color though. He was white when he was a calf. But he turned blue standin' out in the field for six days the first winter of the Blue Snow, and he never got white again. Winter and summer he was always the same, except prob'ly in July—somewheres about the Fourth—he might maybe've been a shade lighter then.

I've heard some of the old loggers say that Paul brought him from Canada when he was a little calf a few days old—carried him across Lake Champlain in a sack so he wouldn't have to pay duty on him. But I'm thinkin' he must of been a mighty few days old at the time or Paul couldn't of done it, for he must of grown pretty fast when he got started, to grow to the size he did. And then besides there's them that says Paul never had him at all when he was a little fellow like that, but that he was a pretty fair sized calf when Paul got him. A fellow by the name of O'Regan down near Detroit is supposed to of had him first. O'Regan didn't have no more'n about forty acres or so under cultivation cleared on his farm and naturally that wasn't near enough to raise feed for Babe, and so he's supposed to of sold him the year of the Short Oats to Paul Bunyan. I don't know exactly. It's all before my time. When I went to work for Paul, and all the time I knowed him, the Ox was full grown.

Babe was as strong as the breath of a tote-teamster, Paul always said, and he could haul a whole section of timber with him at a time—Babe'd walk right off with

it—the entire six hundred forty acres at one drag, and haul it down to the landin' and dump it in. That's why there ain't no section thirty-seven no more. Six trips a day six days a week just cleaned up a township, and the last load they never bothered to haul back Saturday night, but left it lay on the landin' to float away in the spring, and that's why there quit bein' section 37's, and you never see 'em on the maps no more.

The only time I ever saw Babe on a job that seemed to nearly stump him—but that sure did look like it was goin' to for awhile, though—durin' all the time I was with Paul was one time in Wisconsin, down on the St. Croix. And that was when he used him to pull the crooks out of eighteen miles of loggin' road; that come pretty near bein' more'n the Ox could handle. For generally anything that had two ends to it Babe could walk off with like nothin'.

But that road of all the crooked roads I ever see—and I've seen a good many in my day—was of all of 'em the crookedest, and it's no wonder it was pretty near too much for Babe. You won't believe me when I tell you, but it's the truth, that in that stretch of eighteen miles that road doubled back on itself no less than sixteen times, and made four figure 8's, nine 3's, and four S's, yes, and one each of pretty near every other letter in the alphabet.

Of course the trouble with that road was, there was too much of it, and it didn't know what to do with itself, and so it's no wonder it got into mischief.

You'd be walkin' along it, all unsuspectin', and here of a sudden you'd see a coil of it layin' behind a tree, that you never knowed was there, and layin' there lookin' like it was ready to spring at you. The teamsters met themselves comin' back so many times while drivin' over it,

that it begun to get on their nerves and we come near havin' a crazy-house in camp there. And so Paul made up his mind that that there road was goin' to be straightened out right then and there, and he went after it accordin'.

What he done was, he went out and told Bill to bring up the Blue Ox right away, and hitch him to the near end of the road.

Then he went up and spoke somethin' kind of low to Babe, and then afterwards he went out kind of to one side himself, and Babe laid hold, and then is the time it come pretty near breakin' the Ox in two, like I said.

"Come on, Babe! Co-ome on, Ba-abe!" says Paul, and the Ox lays hold and pulls to the last ounce of him. If I live to be a hundred years old I never hope to see an ox pull like that again. His hind legs laid straight out behind him nearly, and his belly was almost down touchin' the ground.

It was one beeg job, as the Frenchmen would of said. And when the crooks finally was all out of that there piece of road, there was enough of it to lay around a round lake we skidded logs into that winter, and then there was enough left in the place where it'd been at first to reach from one end to the other.

I've always been glad I saw Babe on that pull, for it's the greatest thing I ever saw him do—in its way, anyway.

Bill, that took care of the Blue Ox, generally went by the name of Brimstone Bill at camp and the reason was because he got to be so awfully red-hot tempered. But I never blamed him, though. Havin' that Ox to take care of was enough to make a sinner out of the best fellow that ever lived. Of all the scrapin' and haulin' you'd have to do to keep him lookin' anywheres near respectable even, no one would ever think.

And the way he ate—it took two men just to pick the balin' wire out of his teeth at mealtimes. Four ton of grain wasn't nothin' for Babe to get away with at a single meal, and for the hay—I can't mention quantities, but I know they said at first, before he got Windy Knight onto cuttin' it up for nails to use in puttin' on the cook-house roof, Paul used to have to move the camp every two weeks to get away from the mess of haywire that got collected where Babe ate his dinner. And as for cleanin' the barn and haulin' the manure away—

I remember one night in our bunkhouse as plain as if it'd been yesterday. I can see it all again just like it was then. That was one time afterwards, when we was loggin' down in Wisconsin.

There was a new fellow just come to camp that day,

a kind of college fellow that'd come to the woods for his health, and we was all sittin' around the stove that night spinnin' yarns like we almost always done of an evenin' while our socks was dryin'. I was over on one end, and to each side of me was Joe Stiles, and Pat O'Henry—it's funny how I remember it all—and a fellow by the name of Horn, and Big Gus, and a number of others that I don't recollect now, and over on the other end opposite me was Brimstone Bill, and up by me was this new fellow, but kind of a little to the side.

Well, quite a number of stories had been told, and some of 'em had been about the Blue Ox and different experiences men'd had with him different times and how the manure used to pile up, and pretty soon that there college chap begun to tell a story he said it reminded him of—one of them there old ancient Greek stories, he said it was, about Herukles cleanin' the Augaen stables, that was one of twelve other hard jobs he'd been set to do by the king he was workin' for at the time, to get his daughter or somethin' like that. He was goin' at it kind of fancy, describin' how the stables hadn't been cleaned for some time, and what a condition they was in as a consequence, and what a strong man Herukles was, and how he adopted the plan of turnin' the river right through the stables and so washin' the manure away that way, and goin' on describin' how it was all done. And how the water come through and floated the manure all up on top of the river, and how there was enough of it to spread over a whole valley, and then how the manure rolled up in waves again in the river when it got to where it was swifter—and it was a pretty good story and he was quite a talker too, that young fellow was, and he had all the men listenin' to him.

Well, all the time old Brimstone Bill he sat there takin' it all in, and I could see by the way his jaw was workin' on his tobacco that he was gettin' pretty riled. Everythin' had been quiet while the young fellow was tellin' the story, and some of us was smokin', some of us enjoyin' a little fresh Star or Peerless maybe and spittin' in the sandbox occasionally which was gettin' pretty wet by this time, and there wasn't no sound at all except the occasional sizzle when somebody hit the stove, or the movin' of a bench when somebody's foot or sock would get too near the fire, and the man's voice goin' along describin' about this Herukles and how great he was and how fine the stables looked when he got through with 'em, when all at once Brimstone Bill he busted right into him:

"You shut your blamed mouth about that Herik Lees of yourn," he says. "I guess if your Herik Lees had had the job I've got for a few days, he wouldn't of done it so easy or talked so smart, you young Smart Alec, you—" and then a long string of 'em the way Bill could roll 'em off when he got mad—I never heard any much better'n him—they said he could keep goin' for a good half hour and never repeat the same word twict—but I wouldn't give much for a lumberjack who couldn't roll off a few dozen straight—specially if he's worked with cattle—and all the time he was gettin' madder'n madder till he was fairly sizzlin' he was so mad. "I guess if that Mr. Lees had had Babe to take care of he wouldn't of done it so easy. Tell him he can trade jobs with me for a spell if he wants to, and see how he likes it. I guess if he'd of had to use his back on them one hundred and fifty jacks to jack up the barn the way I got to do he wouldn't of had enough strength left in him to brag so much about it. I just got through raisin' it another sixty foot this afternoon. When this job started we was workin' on the level, and now already Babe's barn is up sixteen hundred foot. I'd like to see the river that could wash that pile of manure away, and you can just tell that Herik Lees to come on and try it if he wants to. And if he can't, why then you can just shut up about it. I've walked the old Ox and cleaned 'im and doctored 'im and rubbed 'im ever since he was first invented, and I know what it is, and I ain't goin' to sit here and let you tell me about any Mr. Lees or any other blankety blank liar that don't know what he's talkin' about tellin' about cleanin' barns—not if I know it." And at it he goes again blankety blank blank all the way out through the door, and slams it behind him so the whole bunkhouse shook, and the stranger he sits there and don't know hardly what to make of it. Till I kind of explained to him afterwards before we turned in, and we all, the rest of 'em too, told him not to mind about Bill, for he couldn't hardly help it. After he'd been in camp a few days he'd know. You couldn't hardly blame Bill for bein' aggravated—used to be a real good-natured man, and he wasn't so bad even that time I was helpin' him, but the Ox was too much for any man, no matter who.

THE RAVEN AND THE GOOSE

An Inuit Legend

KNUD RASMUSSEN

Do you know why the raven is so black, so dull and black in colour? It is all because of its own obstinacy. Now listen.

It happened in the days when all the birds were getting their colours and the pattern in their coats. And the raven and the goose happened to meet, and they agreed to paint each other.

The raven began, and painted the other black, with a nice white pattern showing between.

The goose thought that very fine indeed, and began to do the same by the raven, painting it a coat exactly like its own.

But then the raven fell into a rage, and declared the pattern was frightfully ugly, and the goose, offended at all the fuss, simply splashed it black all over.

And now you know why the raven is black.

THE FIRE-BIRD, THE HORSE OF POWER AND THE PRINCESS VASILISSA

A Russian Fairytale

ARTHUR RANSOME

Once upon a time a strong and powerful Tzar ruled in a country far away. And among his servants was a young archer, and this archer had a horse—a horse of power— such a horse as belonged to the wonderful men of long ago—a great horse with a broad chest, eyes like fire, and hoofs of iron. There are no such horses nowadays. They sleep with the strong men who rode them, the bogatirs, until the time comes when Russia has need of them. Then the great horses will thunder up from under the ground, and the valiant men leap from the graves in the armour they have worn so long. The strong men will sit those horses of power, and there will be swinging of clubs and thunder of hoofs, and the earth will be swept clean from the enemies of God and the Tzar. So my grandfather used to say, and he was as much older than I as I am older than you, little ones, and so he should know.

Well, one day long ago, in the green time of the year, the young archer rode through the forest on his horse of power. The trees were green; there were little blue flowers on the ground under the trees; the squirrels ran in the branches, and the hares in the undergrowth;

79

but no birds sang. The young archer rode along the forest path and listened for the singing of the birds, but there was no singing. The forest was silent, and the only noises in it were the scratching of four-footed beasts, the dropping of fir cones, and the heavy stamping of the horse of power in the soft path.

"What has come to the birds?" said the young archer.

He had scarcely said this before he saw a big curving feather lying in the path before him. The feather was larger than a swan's, larger than an eagle's. It lay in the path, glittering like a flame; for the sun was on it, and it was a feather of pure gold. Then he knew why there was no singing in the forest. For he knew that the fire-bird had flown that way, and that the feather in the path before him was a feather from its burning breast.

The horse of power spoke and said:

"Leave the golden feather where it lies. If you take it you will be sorry for it, and know the meaning of fear."

But the brave young archer sat on the horse of power and looked at the golden feather, and wondered whether to take it or not. He had no wish to learn what it was to be afraid, but he thought, "If I take it and bring it to the Tzar my master, he will be pleased; and he will not send me away with empty hands, for no tzar in the world has a feather from the burning breast of the fire-bird." And the more he thought, the more he wanted to carry the feather to the Tzar. And in the end he did not listen to the words of the horse of power. He leapt from the saddle, picked up the golden feather of the fire-bird, mounted his horse again, and galloped back through the green forest till he came to the palace of the Tzar.

He went into the palace, and bowed before the Tzar and said:

"O Tzar, I have brought you a feather of the fire-bird."

The Tzar looked gladly at the feather, and then at the young archer.

"Thank you," says he; "but if you have brought me a feather of the fire-bird, you will be able to bring me the bird itself. I should like to see it. A feather is not a fit gift to bring to the Tzar. Bring the bird itself, or, I swear by my sword, your head shall no longer sit between your shoulders "

The young archer bowed his head and went out. Bitterly he wept, for he knew now what it was to be afraid. He went out into the courtyard, where the horse of power was waiting for him, tossing its head and stamping on the ground.

"Master," says the horse of power, "why do you weep?"

"The Tzar has told me to bring him the fire-bird, and no man on earth can do that," says the young archer, and he bowed his head on his breast.

"I told you," says the horse of power, "that if you took the feather you would learn the meaning of fear. Well, do not be frightened yet, and do not weep. The trouble is not now; the trouble lies before you. Go to the Tzar and ask him to have a hundred sacks of maize scattered over the open field, and let this be done at midnight."

The young archer went back into the palace and begged the Tzar for this, and the Tzar ordered that at midnight a hundred sacks of maize should be scattered in the open field.

Next morning, at the first redness in the sky, the young archer rode out on the horse of power, and came to the open field. The ground was scattered all over with maize. In the middle of the field stood a great oak with spreading boughs. The young archer leapt to the ground, took off the saddle, and let the horse of power loose to wander as he pleased about the field. Then he climbed up into the oak and hid himself among the green boughs.

The sky grew red and gold, and the sun rose. Suddenly there was a noise in the forest round the field. The trees shook and swayed, and almost fell. There was a mighty wind. The sea piled itself into waves with crests of foam, and the fire-bird came flying from the other side of the world. Huge and golden and flaming in the sun, it flew, dropped down with open wings into the field, and began to eat the maize.

The horse of power wandered in the field. This way he went, and that, but always he came a little nearer to the fire-bird. Nearer and nearer came the horse. He came close up to the fire-bird, and then suddenly stepped on one of its spreading fiery wings and pressed it heavily to the ground. The bird struggled, flapping mightily with its fiery wings, but it could not get away. The young archer slipped down from the tree, bound the fire-bird with three strong ropes, swung it on his back, saddled the horse, and rode to the palace of the Tzar.

The young archer stood before the Tzar, and his back was bent under the great weight of the fire-bird, and the broad wings of the bird hung on either side of him like fiery shields, and there was a trail of golden feathers on the floor. The young archer swung the magic bird to the foot of the throne before the Tzar; and the Tzar was glad, because since the beginning of the world no Tzar had seen the fire-bird flung before him like a wild duck caught in a snare.

The Tzar looked at the fire-bird and laughed with pride. Then he lifted his eyes and looked at the young archer, and says he:

"As you have known how to take the fire-bird, you will know how to bring me my bride, for whom I have long been waiting. In the land of Never, on the very edge of the world, where the red sun rises in flame from behind the sea, lives the Princess Vasilissa. I will marry none but her. Bring her to me, and I will reward you with silver and gold. But if you do not bring her, then, by my sword, your head will no longer sit between your shoulders!"

The young archer wept bitter tears, and went out into the courtyard where the horse of power was stamping the ground with its hoofs of iron and tossing its thick mane.

"Master, why do you weep?" asked the horse of power.

"The Tzar has ordered me to go to the land of Never, and to bring back the Princess Vasilissa."

"Do not weep—do not grieve. The trouble is not yet; the trouble is to come. Go to the Tzar and ask him for a silver tent with a golden roof, and for all kinds of food and drink to take with us on the journey."

The young archer went in and asked the Tzar for this, and the Tzar gave him a silver tent with silver hangings and a gold-embroidered roof, and every kind of rich wine and the tastiest of foods.

Then the young archer mounted the horse of power and rode off to the land of Never. On and on he rode, many days and nights, and came at last to the edge of the world, where the red sun rises in flame from behind the deep blue sea.

On the shore of the sea the young archer reined in the horse of power, and the heavy hoofs of the horse sank in the sand. He shaded his eyes and looked out over the blue water, and there was the Princess Vasilissa in a little silver boat, rowing with golden oars.

The young archer rode back a little way to where the sand ended and the green world began. There he loosed the horse to wander where he pleased, and to feed on the green grass. Then on the edge of the shore, where the green grass ended and grew thin and the sand began, he set up the shining tent, with its silver hangings and its gold-embroidered roof. In the tent he set out the tasty dishes and the rich flagons of wine which the Tzar had given him, and he sat himself down in the tent and began to regale himself, while he waited for the Princess Vasilissa.

The Princess Vasilissa dipped her golden oars in the blue water, and the little silver boat moved lightly through the dancing waves. She sat in the little boat and looked over the blue sea to the edge of the world, and there, between the golden sand and the green earth, she saw the tent standing, silver and gold in the sun. She dipped her oars, and came nearer to see it better. The nearer she came the fairer seemed the tent, and at last she rowed to the shore and grounded her little boat on the golden sand, and stepped out daintily and came up to the tent. She was a little frightened, and now and again she stopped and looked back to where the silver boat lay on the sand with the blue sea beyond it. The young archer said not a word, but went on regaling himself on the pleasant dishes he had set out there in the tent.

At last the Princess Vasilissa came up to the tent and looked in.

The young archer rose and bowed before her. Says he:

"Good day to you, Princess! Be so kind as to come in and take bread and salt with me, and taste my foreign wines."

And the Princess Vasilissa came into the tent and sat down with the young archer, and ate sweetmeats with him, and drank his health in a golden goblet of the wine the Tzar had given him. Now this wine was heavy, and the last drop from the goblet had no sooner trickled down her little slender throat than her eyes closed against her will, once, twice, and again.

"Ah me!" says the Princess, "it is as if the night itself had perched on my eyelids, and yet it is but noon."

And the golden goblet dropped to the ground from her little fingers, and she leant back on a cushion and fell instantly asleep. If she had been beautiful before, she was lovelier still when she lay in that deep sleep in the shadow of the tent.

Quickly the young archer called to the horse of power. Lightly he lifted the Princess in his strong young arms. Swiftly he leapt with her into the saddle. Like a feather she lay in the hollow of his left arm, and slept while the iron hoofs of the great horse thundered over the ground.

They came to the Tzar's palace, and the young archer leapt from the horse of power and carried the Princess into the palace. Great was the joy of the Tzar; but it did not last for long.

"Go, sound the trumpets for our wedding," he said to his servants, "let all the bells be rung."

The bells rang out and the trumpets sounded, and at the noise of the horns and the ringing of the bells the Princess Vasilissa woke up and looked about her.

"What is this ringing of bells," says she, "and this noise of trumpets? And where, oh, where is the blue sea, and my little silver boat with its golden oars?" And the Princess put her hand to her eyes.

"The blue sea is far away," says the Tzar, "and for your little silver boat I give you a golden throne. The trumpets sound for our wedding, and the bells are ringing for our joy."

But the Princess turned her face away from the Tzar; and there was no wonder in that, for he was old, and his eyes were not kind.

And she looked with love at the young archer; and there was no wonder in that either, for he was a young man fit to ride the horse of power.

The Tzar was angry with the Princess Vasilissa, but his anger was as useless as his joy.

"Why, Princess," says he, "will you not marry me, and forget your blue sea and your silver boat?"

"In the middle of the deep blue sea lies a great stone,"

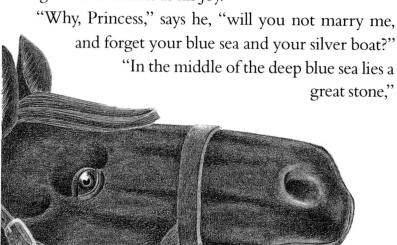

says the Princess, "and under that stone is hidden my wedding-dress. If I cannot wear that dress I will marry nobody at all."

Instantly the Tzar turned to the young archer, who was waiting before the throne.

"Ride swiftly back," says he, "to the land of Never, where the red sun rises in flame. There—do you hear what the Princess says?—a great stone lies in the middle of the sea. Under that stone is hidden her wedding-dress. Ride swiftly. Bring back that dress, or, by my sword, your head shall no longer sit between your shoulders!"

The young archer wept bitter tears, and went out into the courtyard, where the horse of power was waiting for him, champing its golden bit.

"There is no way of escaping death this time," he said.

"Master, why do you weep?" asked the horse of power.

"The Tzar has ordered me to ride to the land of Never, to fetch the wedding-dress of the Princess Vasilissa from the bottom of the deep blue sea. Besides, the dress is wanted for the Tzar's wedding, and I love the Princess myself."

"What did I tell you?" says the horse of power. "I told you that there would be trouble if you picked up the golden feather from the fire-bird's burning breast. Well, do not be afraid. The trouble is not yet; the trouble is to come. Up! Into the saddle with you, and away for the wedding-dress of the Princess Vasilissa!"

The young archer leapt into the saddle, and the horse of power, with his thundering hoofs, carried him swiftly through the green forests and over the bare plains, till they came to the edge of the world, to the land of Never, where the red sun rises in flame from behind the deep blue sea. There they rested, at the very edge of the sea.

The young archer looked sadly over the wide waters, but the horse of power tossed its mane and did not look at the sea, but on the shore. This way and that it looked, and saw at last a huge lobster moving slowly, sideways, along the golden sand.

Nearer and nearer came the lobster, and it was a giant among lobsters, the tzar of all the lobsters; and it moved slowly along the shore, while the horse of power moved carefully and as if by accident, until it stood between the lobster and the sea. Then when the lobster came close by, the horse of power lifted an iron hoof and set it firmly on the lobster's tail.

"You will be the death of me!" screamed the lobster—as well he might, with the heavy foot of the horse of power pressing his tail into the sand. "Let me live, and I will do whatever you ask of me."

"Very well," says the horse of power, "we will let you live" and he slowly lifted his foot. "But this is what you shall do for us. In the middle of the blue sea lies a great stone, and under that stone is hidden the wedding-dress of the Princess Vasilissa. Bring it here."

The lobster groaned with the pain in his tail. Then he cried out in a voice that could be heard all over the deep blue sea. And the sea was disturbed, and from all sides lobsters in thousands made their way towards the bank. And the huge lobster that was the oldest of them all and the tzar of all the lobsters that live between the rising and the setting of the sun, gave them the order and sent them back into the sea. And the young archer sat on the horse of power and waited.

After a little time the sea was disturbed again, and the lobsters in their thousands came to the shore, and with them they brought a golden casket in which was the wedding-dress of the Princess Vasilissa. They had taken it from under the great stone that lay in the middle of the sea.

The tzar of all the lobsters raised himself painfully on his bruised tail and gave the casket into the hands of the young archer, and instantly the horse of power turned himself about and galloped back to the palace of the Tzar, far, far away, at the other side of the green forests and beyond the treeless plains.

The young archer went into the palace and gave the casket into the hands of the Princess, and looked at her with sadness in his eyes, and she looked at him with love. Then she went away into an inner chamber, and came back in her wedding-dress, fairer than the spring itself. Great was the joy of the Tzar. The wedding feast was made ready, and the bells rang, and flags waved above the palace.

The Tzar held out his hand to the Princess, and looked at her with his old eyes. But she would not take his hand.

"No," says she, "I will marry nobody until the man who brought me here has done penance in boiling water."

Instantly the Tzar turned to his servants and ordered them to make a great fire, and to fill a great cauldron with water and set it on the fire, and, when the water should be at its hottest, to take the young archer and throw him into it, to do penance for having taken the Princess Vasilissa away from the land of Never.

There was no gratitude in the mind of that Tzar.

Swiftly the servants brought wood and made a mighty fire, and on it they laid a huge cauldron of water, and built the fire round the walls of the cauldron. The fire burned hot and the water steamed. The fire burned hotter, and the water bubbled and seethed. They made ready to take the young archer, to throw him into the cauldron.

"Oh, misery!" thought the young archer. "Why did I ever take the golden feather that had fallen from the fire-bird's burning breast? Why did I not listen to the wise words of the horse of power?" And he remembered the horse of power, and he begged the Tzar:

"O lord Tzar, I do not complain. I shall presently die in the heat of the water on the fire. Suffer me, before I die, once more to see my horse."

"Let him see his horse," says the Princess.

"Very well," says the Tzar. "Say good-bye to your horse, for you will not ride him again. But let your farewells be short, for we are waiting."

The young archer crossed the courtyard and came to the horse of power, who was scraping the ground with his iron hoofs.

"Farewell, my horse of power," says the young archer. "I should have listened to your words of wisdom, for now the end is come, and we shall never more see the green trees pass above us and the ground disappear beneath us, as we race the wind between the earth and the sky."

"Why so?" says the horse of power.

"The Tzar has ordered that I am to be boiled to death—thrown into that cauldron that is seething on the great fire."

"Fear not," says the horse of power, "for the Princess Vasilissa has made him do this, and the end of these things is better than I thought. Go back, and when they are ready to throw you in the cauldron, do you run boldly and leap yourself into the boiling water."

The young archer went back across the courtyard, and the servants made ready to throw him into the cauldron.

"Are you sure that the water is boiling?" says the Princess Vasilissa.

"It bubbles and seethes," said the servants.

"Let me see for myself," says the Princess, and she went to the fire and waved her hand above the cauldron. And some say there was something in her hand, and some say there was not.

"It is boiling," says she, and the servants laid hands on the young archer; but he threw them from him, and ran and leapt boldly before them all into the very middle of the cauldron.

Twice he sank below the surface, borne round with the bubbles and foam of the boiling water. Then he leapt from the cauldron and stood before the Tzar and the Princess. He had become so beautiful a youth that all who saw cried aloud in wonder.

"This is a miracle," says the Tzar. And the Tzar looked at the beautiful young archer, and thought of himself—of his age, of his bent back, and his grey beard, and his toothless gums. "I too will become beautiful," thinks he, and he rose from his throne and clambered into the cauldron, and was boiled to death in a moment.

And the end of the story? They buried the Tzar, and made the young archer Tzar in his place. He married the Princess Vasilissa, and lived many years with her in love and good fellowship. And he built a golden stable for the horse of power, and never forgot what he owed to him.

HOW THE RABBIT LOST HIS TAIL

A Native American Legend

CYRUS MACMILLAN

When Glooskap first created the animals in Canada, he took good care that they should all be friendly to himself and to his people. They could all talk like men, and like them they had one common speech. Each had a special duty to do for Glooskap, and each did his best to help him in his work. Of all the animals, the gentlest and most faithful was Bunny the Rabbit. Now, in those first days of his life, Rabbit was a very beautiful animal, more beautiful than he is to-day. He had a very long bushy tail like a fox; he always wore a thick brown coat; his body was large and round and sleek; his legs were straight and strong; he walked and ran like other animals and did not hop and jump about as he does now. He was always very polite and kind of heart. Because of his beauty and his good qualities, Glooskap chose him as his forest guide, his Scout of the Woods. He gave him power that enabled him to know well all the land, so that he could lead people and all the other animals wherever they wished to go without losing their way.

One day in the springtime it chanced that Bunny sat alone on a log in the forest, his long bushy tail trailing far

behind him. He had just come back from a long scouting tour and he was very tired. As he sat resting in the sun, an Indian came along. The Indian was weary and stained with much travel, and he looked like a wayfarer who had come far. He threw himself on the ground close to the log on which Rabbit sat and began to weep bitterly. Bunny with his usual kindness asked, "Why do you weep?" And the man answered, "I have lost my way in the forest. I am on my way to marry this afternoon a beautiful girl whom her father pledged to me long ago. She is loved by a wicked forest Fairy and I have heard that perhaps she loves him. And I know that if I am late she will refuse to wait for me and that she will marry him instead." But Rabbit said: "Have no fear. I am Bunny, Glooskap's forest guide. I will show you the way and bring you to the wedding in good time." The man was comforted and his spirits rose, and they talked some time together and became good friends.

When the man had somewhat got back his strength, they began their journey to the wedding. But Rabbit, being nimble-footed, ran fast and was soon so far in advance of his companion that he was lost to view. The man followed slowly, catching here and there through the

green trees a glimpse of his guide's brown coat. As he stumbled along, thinking of his troubles, he fell into a deep pit that lay close to the forest path. He was too weak to climb out, and he called loudly for help. Bunny soon missed his follower, but he heard the man's yells, and turning about he ran back to the pit. "Have no fear," said the Rabbit as he looked over the edge, "I will get you out without mishap." Then, turning his back to the pit, he let his long bushy tail hang to the bottom. "Catch hold of my tail," he ordered, "hold on tight and I will pull you out." The man did as he was told. Rabbit sprang forward, but as he jumped, the weight of the man, who was very heavy, was more than he could bear, and poor Bunny's tail broke off within an inch of the root. The man fell back into the pit with a thud, holding in his hand poor Rabbit's tail. But Bunny in all his work as a guide had never known defeat, and he determined not to know it now. Holding to a strong tree with his front feet, he put his hind legs into the pit and said to the man, "Take hold of my legs and hang on tight." The man did as he was told. Then Rabbit pulled and pulled until his hind legs stretched and he feared that they too would break off; but although the weight on them was great, he finally pulled the man out after great difficulty. He found to his dismay that his hind legs had lengthened greatly because of their heavy load. He was no longer able to walk straight, but he now had to hop along with a strange jumping gait. Even his body was much stretched, and his waist had become very slender because of his long heavy pull. The two travellers then went on their way, Bunny hopping along, and the man moving more cautiously.

Finally, they reached the end of their journey. The people were all gathered for the wedding, and eagerly awaiting the coming of the bridegroom. Sure enough, the forest Fairy was there, trying by his tricks to win the girl for himself. But the man was in good time, and he married the maiden as he had hoped. As he was very thankful to Bunny, he asked him to the marriage dance and told him he might dance with the bride. So Rabbit put rings on his heels and a bangle around his neck, after his usual custom at weddings, and joined the merry-makers. Through the forest green where they danced many tiny streams were flowing, and to the soft music of these the dance went on. As the bride jumped across one of these streams during her dance with Bunny, she accidentally let the end of her dress drop into the water so that it got very wet. When she moved again into the sun, her dress, because of its wetting, shrank and shrank until it reached her knees and made her much ashamed. But Rabbit's heart was touched as usual by her plight; he ran quickly and got a deer skin that he knew to be hidden in the trees not far away, and he wrapped the pretty skin around the bride. Then he twisted a cord with which to tie it on. He held one end of the cord in his teeth and twisted the other end with his front paws. But in his haste, he held it so tight and twisted it so hard that when a couple waltzing past carelessly bumped into him the cord split his upper lip right up to the nose. But Rabbit was not dismayed by his split lip. He fastened on the bride's new deer-skin gown, and then he danced all the evening until the moon was far up in the sky. Before he went away, the man and his bride wanted to pay him for his work, but he would not take payment. Then the bride gave him a new white fur coat and said, "In winter wear this white coat; it is the colour of snow; your enemies cannot then see you so plainly against the white ground, and they cannot so easily do you harm; but in summer wear your old brown coat, the colour of the leaves and grass." And Bunny gratefully took the coat and went his way.

He lingered many days in the new country, for he was ashamed to go back to his own people with his changed appearance. His lip was split; his tail was gone, and his hind legs were stretched and crooked. Finally, he mustered up his courage and returned home. His old friends wondered much at his changed looks, and some of then were cruel enough to laugh at him. But Bunny deceived them all. When they asked him where he had been so long, he answered, "I guided a man to a far-off land which you have never seen and of which you have never heard." Then he told them many strange tales of its beauty and its good people.

"How did you lose your fine tail?" they asked. And he answered, "In the land to which I have been, the animals wear no tails. It is an aristocratic country, and wishing to be in the fashion, I cut mine off."

"And why is your waist so slender?" they asked. "Oh," replied Bunny, "in that country it is not the fashion to be fat, and I took great trouble to make my waist slight and willowy." "Why do you hop about," they asked, "when you once walked so straight?" "In that land," answered Bunny, "it is not genteel to walk straight; only the vulgar and untrained do that. The best people have a walk of their own, and it took me many days under a good walking-teacher to learn it."

"But how did you split your upper lip?" they asked finally. "In the land to which I have been," said Bunny, "the people do not eat as we do. There they eat with knives and forks and not with their paws. I found it hard to get used to their new ways. One day I put food into my mouth with my knife—a very vulgar act in that land—and my knife slipped and cut my lip, and the wound has never healed."

And being deceived and envying Bunny because of the wonders he had seen, they asked him no more questions. But the descendants of Rabbit to this day wear a white coat in winter and a brown one in summer. They have also a split upper lip; their waist is still very slender; they have no tail; their hind legs are longer than their front ones; they hop and jump nimbly about, but they are unable to walk straight. And all these strange things are a result of old Bunny's accident at the man's wedding long ago.

HOW SOME WILD ANIMALS BECAME TAME ONES

A Lapp Fairytale

ANDREW LANG

Once upon a time there lived a miller who was so rich that, when he was going to be married, he asked to the feast not only his own friends but also the wild animals who dwelt in the hills and woods round about. The chief of the bears, the wolves, the foxes, the horses, the cows, the goats, the sheep, and the reindeer, all received invitations; and as they were not accustomed to weddings they were greatly pleased and flattered, and sent back messages in the politest language that they would certainly be there.

The first to start on the morning of the wedding-day was the bear, who always liked to be punctual; and, besides,

he had a long way to go, and his hair, being so thick and rough, needed a good brushing before it was fit to be seen at a party. However, he took care to awaken very early, and set off down the road with a light heart. Before he had walked very far he met a boy who came whistling along, hitting at the tops of the flowers with a stick.

"Where are you going?" said he, looking at the bear in surprise, for he was an old acquaintance, and not generally so smart.

"Oh, just to the miller's marriage," answered the bear carelessly. "Of course, I would much rather stay at home, but the miller was so anxious I should be there that I really could not refuse."

"Don't go, don't go!" cried the boy. "If you do you will never come back! You have got the most beautiful skin in the world—just the kind that everyone is wanting, and they will be sure to kill you and strip you of it."

"I had not thought of that," said the bear, whose face turned white, only nobody could see it. "If you are certain that they would be so wicked—but perhaps you are jealous because nobody has invited *you*?"

"Oh, nonsense!" replied the boy angrily, "do as you see fit. It is your skin, and not mine; *I* don't care what becomes of it!" And he walked quickly on with his head in the air.

The bear waited until he was out of sight, and then followed him slowly, for he felt in his heart that the boy's advice was good, though he was too proud to say so.

The boy soon grew tired of walking along the road, and turned off into the woods, where there were bushes he could jump and streams he could wade; but he had not gone far before he met the wolf.

"Where are you going?" asked he, for it was not the first time he had seen him.

"Oh, just to the miller's marriage," answered the wolf, as the bear had done before him. "It is rather tiresome, of course—weddings are always so stupid; but still one must be good-natured!"

"Don't go!" said the boy again. "Your skin is so thick and warm, and winter is not far off now. They will kill you, and strip it from you."

The wolf's jaw dropped in astonishment and terror. "Do you *really* think that would happen?" he gasped.

"Yes, to be sure, I do," answered the boy. "But it is your affair, not mine. So good-morning," and on he went. The wolf stood still for a few minutes, for he was trembling all over, and then crept quietly back to his cave.

Next the boy met the fox whose lovely coat of silvery grey was shining in the sun.

"You look very fine!" said the boy, stopping to admire him, "are you going to the miller's wedding too?"

"Yes," answered the fox; "it is a long journey to take for such a thing as that, but you know what the miller's friends are like—so dull and heavy! It is only kind to go and amuse them a little."

"You poor fellow," said the boy pityingly. "Take my advice and stay at home. If you once enter the miller's gate his dogs will tear you in pieces."

"Ah, well, such things *have* occurred, I know," replied the fox gravely. And without saying any more he trotted off the way he had come.

His tail had scarcely disappeared, when a great noise of crashing branches was heard, and up bounded the horse, his black skin glistening like satin.

"Good-morning," he called to the boy as he galloped past, "I can't wait to talk to you. I have promised the miller to be present at his wedding-feast, and they won't sit down till I come."

"Stop! stop!" cried the boy after him, and there was something in his voice that made the horse pull up. "What is the matter?" asked he.

"You don't know what you are doing," said the boy. "If once you go there you will never gallop through these woods any more. You are stronger than many men, but they will catch you and put ropes around you, and you will have to work and to serve them all the days of your life."

The horse threw back his head at these words, and laughed scornfully.

"Yes, I am stronger than many men," answered he,

"and all the ropes in the world would not hold me. Let them bind me as fast as they will, I can always break loose, and return to the forest and freedom."

And with this proud speech he gave a whisk of his long tail, and galloped away faster than before.

But when he reached the miller's house everything happened as the boy had said. While he was looking at the guests and thinking how much handsomer and stronger he was than any of them, a rope was suddenly flung over his head, and he was thrown down and a bit thrust between his teeth. Then, in spite of his struggles, he was dragged to a stable, and shut up for several days without any food, till his spirit was broken and his coat had lost its gloss. After that he was harnessed to a plough, and had plenty of time to remember all he had lost through not listening to the counsel of the boy.

When the horse had turned a deaf ear to his words the boy wandered idly along, sometimes gathering wild strawberries from a bank, and sometimes plucking wild cherries from a tree, till he reached a clearing in the middle of the forest. Crossing this open space was a beautiful milk-white cow with a wreath of flowers round her neck.

"Good-morning," she said pleasantly, as she came up to the place where the boy was standing.

"Good-morning," he returned. "Where are you going in such a hurry?"

"To the miller's wedding; I am rather late already, for the wreath took such a long time to make, so I can't stop."

"Don't go," said the boy earnestly; "when once they have tasted your milk they will never let you leave them, and you will have to serve them all the days of your life."

"Oh, nonsense; what do *you* know about it?" answered the cow, who always thought she was wiser than other people. "Why, I can run twice as fast as any of them! I should like to see anybody try to keep me against my will." And, without even a polite bow, she went on her way, feeling very much offended.

But everything turned out just as the boy had said. The company had all heard of the fame of the cow's milk, and persuaded her to give them some, and then her doom was sealed. A crowd gathered round her, and held her horns so that she could not use them, and, like the horse, she was shut in the stable, and only let out in the mornings, when a long rope was tied round her head, and she was fastened to a stake in a grassy meadow.

And so it happened to the goat and to the sheep.

Last of all came the reindeer, looking as he always did, as if some serious business was on hand.

"Where are you going?" asked the boy, who by this time was tired of wild cherries, and was thinking of his dinner.

"I am invited to the wedding," answered the reindeer, "and the miller has begged me on no account to fail him."

"O fool!" cried the boy, "have you no sense at all? Don't you know that when you get there they will hold you fast, for neither beast no bird is as strong or as swift as you?"

"That is exactly why I am quite safe," replied the reindeer. "I am so strong that no one can bind me, and so swift that not even an arrow can catch me. So, goodbye for the present, you will soon see me back."

But none of the animals that went to the miller's wedding ever came back. And because they were self-willed and conceited, and would not listen to good advice, they and their children have been the servants of men to this very day.

THE RELUCTANT DRAGON

The Boy has made the acquaintance of a most unusual dragon who would rather quote poetry than fight. When the great dragon-hunter St. George comes to town, the Boy must find a way to keep St. George from hurting his dragon friend.

KENNETH GRAHAME

One day the Boy, on walking into the village, found everything wearing a festal appearance which was not to be accounted for in the calendar. Carpets and gay-coloured stuffs were hung out of the windows, the church bells clamoured noisily, the little street was flower-strewn, and the whole population jostled each other along either side of it, chattering, shoving and ordering each other to stand back. The Boy saw a friend of his own age in the crowd and hailed him.

"What's up!" he cried. "Is it the players, or bears, or a circus, or what?"

"It's all right," his friend hailed back. "He's a-coming."

"*Who's* a-coming?" demanded the Boy, thrusting into the throng.

"Why, St. George, of course," replied his friend. "He heard tell of our dragon, and he's comin' on purpose to slay the deadly beast, and free us from his horrid yoke. O my! won't there be a jolly fight!"

Here was news indeed! The Boy felt that he ought to make quite sure for himself, and he wriggled himself in between the legs of his good-natured elders, abusing them all the time for their unmannerly habit of shoving. Once in the front rank, he breathlessly awaited the arrival.

Presently from the faraway end of the line came the sound of cheering. Next, the measured tramp of a great war-horse made his heart beat quicker, and then he found himself cheering with the rest, as, amidst welcoming shouts, shrill cries of women, uplifting of babies and waving of handkerchiefs, St. George paced slowly up the street. The Boy's heart stood still and he breathed with sobs, the beauty and the grace of the hero were so far beyond anything he had yet seen. His fluted armour was inlaid with gold, his plumed helmet hung at his saddlebow, and his thick fair hair framed a face gracious and gentle beyond expression till you caught the sternness in his eyes. He drew rein in front of the little inn, and the villagers crowded round with greetings and thanks and voluble statements of their wrongs and grievances and oppressions. The Boy heard the grave gentle voice of the Saint, assuring them that all would be well now, and that he would stand by them and see then righted and free them from their foe; then he dismounted and passed through the doorway and the crowd poured in after him. But the Boy made off up the hill as fast as he could lay his legs to the ground.

"It's all up, dragon!" he shouted as soon as he was within sight of the beast. "He's coming! He's here now! You'll have to pull yourself together and *do* something at last!"

The dragon was licking his scales and rubbing them with a bit of house-flannel the Boy's mother had lent him, till he shone like a great turquoise.

"Don't be *violent*, Boy," he said without looking

round. "Sit down and get your breath, and try and remember that the noun governs the verb, and then perhaps you'll be good enough to tell me *who's* coming?"

"That's right, take it coolly," said the Boy. "Hope you'll be half as cool when I've got through with my news. It's only St. George who's coming, that's all; he rode into the village half an hour ago. Of course you can lick him— a great big fellow like you! But I thought I'd warn you, 'cos he's sure to be round early, and he's got the longest, wickedest-looking spear you ever did see!" And the Boy got up and began to jump round in sheer delight at the prospect of the battle.

"O deary, deary me," moaned the dragon. "This is too awful. I won't see him, and that's flat. I don't want to know the fellow at all. I'm sure he's not nice. You must tell him to go away at once, please. Say he can write if he likes, but I can't give him an interview. I'm not seeing anybody at present."

"Now dragon, dragon," said the Boy imploringly, "don't be perverse and wrongheaded. You've *got* to fight him sometime or other, you know, 'cos he's St. George and you're the dragon. Better get it over, and then we can go on with the sonnets. And you ought to consider other people a little, too. If it's been dull up here for you, think how dull it's been for me!"

"My dear little man," said the dragon solemnly, "just understand, once for all, that I can't fight and I won't fight. I've never fought in my life, and I'm not going to begin now, just to give you a Roman holiday. In old days I always let the other fellows—the *earnest* fellows—do all the fighting, and no doubt that's why I have the pleasure of being here now."

"But if you don't fight he'll cut your head off!"
gasped the Boy, miserable at the prospect of losing both his
fight and his friend.

"Oh, I think not," said the dragon in his lazy way.
"You'll be able to arrange something. I've every confidence in you, you're such a *manager*. Just run down, there's
a dear chap, and make it all right. I leave it entirely to you."

The Boy pursued his way to the inn, and passed into
the principal chamber, where St. George now sat alone,
musing over the chances of the fight, and the sad stories of
rapine and of wrong that had so lately been poured into
his sympathetic ears.

"May I come in, St. George?" said the Boy
politely, as he paused at the door. "I want to talk to you
about this little matter of the dragon, if you're not tired
of it by this time."

"Yes, come in, Boy," said the Saint kindly. "Another
tale of misery and wrong, I fear me. Is it a kind parent,
then, of whom the tyrant has bereft you? Or some tender
sister or brother? Well, it shall soon be avenged."

"Nothing of the sort," said the Boy. "There's a mis-
understanding somewhere, and I want to put it right. The
fact is, this is a *good* dragon."

"Exactly," said St. George, smiling pleasantly, "I quite
understand. A good *dragon*. Believe me, I do not in the
least regret that he is an adversary worthy of my steel, and
no feeble specimen of his noxious tribe."

"But he's *not* a noxious tribe," cried the Boy dis-
tressedly. "Oh dear, oh dear, how *stupid* men are when
they get an idea into their heads! I tell you he's a *good*
dragon, and a friend of mine, and tells me the most beautiful stories you ever heard, all about old times and when

he was little. And he's been so kind to mother, and mother'd do anything for him. And father likes him too, though father doesn't hold with art and poetry much, and always falls asleep when the dragon starts talking about *style*. But the fact is, nobody can help liking him when once they know him. He's so engaging and so trustful, and as simple as a child!"

"Sit down, and draw your chair up," said St. George. "I like a fellow who sticks up for his friends, and I'm sure the dragon has his good points, if he's got a friend like you. But that's not the question. All this evening I've been listening, with grief and anguish unspeakable, to tales of murder, theft, and wrong; rather too highly coloured, perhaps, not always quite convincing, but forming in the main a most serious roll of crime. History teaches us that the greatest rascals often possess all the domestic virtues; and I fear that your cultivated friend, in spite of the qualities which have won (and rightly) your regard, has got to be speedily exterminated."

"Oh, you've been taking in all the yarns those fellows have been telling you," said the Boy impatiently. "Why, our villagers are the biggest story-tellers in all the country round. It's a known fact. You're a stranger in these parts, or else you'd have heard it already. All they want is a *fight*. They're the most awful beggars for getting up fights—it's meat and drink to them. Dogs, bulls, dragons—anything so long as it's a fight. Why, they've got a poor innocent badger in the stable behind here, at this moment. They were going to have some fun with him today, but they're saving him up now till *your* little affair's over. And I've no doubt they've been telling you what a hero you were, and how you were bound to win, in the cause of right and justice, and so on; but let me tell you, I came down the street just now, and they were betting six to four on the dragon freely!"

"Six to four on the dragon!" murmured St. George sadly, resting his cheek on his hand. "This is an evil world, and sometimes I begin to think that all the wickedness in it is not entirely bottled up inside the dragons. And yet— may not this wily beast have misled you as to his real character, in order that your good report of him may serve as a cloak for his evil deeds? Nay, may there not be, at this very moment, some hapless Princess immured within yonder gloomy cavern?"

The moment he had spoken, St. George was sorry for what he had said, the Boy looked so genuinely distressed.

"I assure you, St. George," he said earnestly, "there's nothing of the sort in the cave at all. The dragon's a real gentleman, every inch of him, and I may say that no one would be more shocked and grieved than he would, at hearing you talk in that—that *loose* way about matters on which he has very strong views!"

"Well, perhaps I've been over-credulous," said St. George. "Perhaps I've misjudged the animal. But what are we to do? Here are the dragon and I, almost face to face, each supposed to be thirsting for each other's blood. I don't see any way out of it, exactly. What do you suggest? Can't you arrange things, somehow?"

"That's just what the dragon said," replied the Boy, rather nettled. "Really, the way you two seem to leave everything to me—I suppose you couldn't be persuaded to go away quietly, could you?"

"Impossible, I fear," said the Saint. "Quite against the rules. *You* know that as well as I do."

"Well, then, look here," said the Boy, "it's early yet— would you mind strolling up with me and seeing the dragon and talking it over? It's not far, and any friend of mine will be most welcome."

"Well, it's *irregular*," said St. George, rising, "but really it seems about the most sensible thing to do. You're taking a lot of trouble on your friend's account," he added, good-naturedly, as they passed out through the door together. "But cheer up! Perhaps there won't have to be any fight after all."

"Oh, but I hope there will, though!" replied the little fellow, wistfully.

"I've brought a friend to see you, dragon," said the Boy, rather loud.

The dragon woke up with a start. "I was just—er—thinking about things," he said in his simple way. "Very pleased to make your acquaintance, sir. Charming weather we're having!"

"This is St. George," said the Boy, shortly. "St. George, let me introduce you to the dragon. We've come up to talk things over quietly, dragon, and now for goodness' sake do let us have a little straight common sense, and come to some practical business-like arrangement, for I'm sick of views and theories of life and personal tendencies, and all that sort of thing. I may perhaps add that my mother's sitting up."

"So glad to meet you, St. George," began the dragon rather nervously, "because you've been a great traveller, I hear and I've always been rather a stay-at-home. But I can show you many antiquities, many interesting features of our countryside, if you're stopping here anytime—"

"I think," said St. George, in his frank, pleasant way, "that we'd really better take the advice of our young friend here, and try to come to some understanding, on a business footing, about this little affair of ours. Now don't you think that after all the simplest plan would be just to fight it out, according to the rules, and let the best man win? They're betting on you, I may tell you, down in the village, but I don't mind that!"

"Oh, yes, *do*, dragon," said the Boy, delightedly. "It'll save such a lot of bother!"

"My young friend, you shut up," said the dragon severely. "Believe me, St. George," he went on, "there's nobody in the world I'd rather oblige than you and this young gentleman here. But the whole thing's nonsense, and conventionality, and popular thick-headedness.

There's absolutely nothing to fight about, from beginning to end. And anyhow I'm not going to, so that settles it!"

"But supposing I make you?" said St. George, rather nettled.

"You can't," said the dragon, triumphantly. "I should only go into my cave and retire for a time down the hole I came up. You'd soon get heartily sick of sitting outside and waiting for me to come out and fight you. And as soon as you'd really gone away, why, I'd come up again gaily, for I tell you frankly, I like this place, and I'm going to stay here!"

St. George gazed for a while on the fair landscape around them. "But this would be a beautiful place for a fight," he began again persuasively. "These great bare rolling Downs for the arena—and me in my golden armour showing up against your big blue scaly coils! Think what a picture it would make!"

"Now you're trying to get at me through my artistic sensibilities," said the dragon. "But it won't work. Not but what it would make a very pretty picture, as you say," he added, wavering a little.

"We seem to be getting rather nearer to *business*," put in the Boy. "You must see, dragon, that there's got to be a fight of some sort, 'cos you can't want to have to go down that dirty old hole again and stop there till goodness knows when."

"It might be arranged," said St. George, thoughtfully. "I *must* spear you somewhere, of course, but I'm not bound to hurt you very much. There's such a lot of you that there must be a few *spare* places somewhere. Here, for instance, just behind your foreleg. It couldn't hurt you much, just here!"

"Now you're tickling, George," said the dragon, coyly. "No, that place won't do at all. Even if it didn't hurt—and I'm sure it would, awfully—it would make me laugh, and that would spoil everything."

"Let's try somewhere else, then," said St. George, patiently. "Under your neck, for instance—all these folds of thick skin—if I speared you here you'd never even know I'd done it!"

"Yes, but are you sure you can hit off the right place?" asked the dragon, anxiously.

"Of course I am," said St. George, with confidence. "You leave that to me!"

"It's just because I've *got* to leave it to you that I'm ·asking," replied the dragon, rather testily. "No doubt you would deeply regret any error you might make in the hurry of the moment; but you wouldn't regret it half as much as I should! However, I suppose we've got to trust somebody, as we go through life, and your plan seems, on the whole, as good a one as any."

"Look here, dragon," interrupted the Boy, a little jealous on behalf of his friend, who seemed to be getting all the worst of the bargain. "I don't quite see where *you* come in! There's to be a fight, apparently, and you're to be licked; and what I want to know is, what are *you* going to get out of it?"

"St. George," said the dragon, "just tell him, please, what will happen after I'm vanquished in the deadly combat?"

"Well, according to the rules I suppose I shall lead you in triumph down to the marketplace or whatever answers to it," said St. George.

"Precisely," said the dragon. "And then—"

"And then there'll be shoutings and speeches and things," continued St. George. "And I shall explain that you're converted, and see the error of your ways, and so on."

"Quite so," said the dragon. "And then—?"

"Oh, and then—" said St. George, "why, and then there will be the usual banquet, I suppose."

"Exactly," said the dragon; "and that's where *I* come in. Look here," he continued, addressing the Boy, "I'm bored to death up here, and no one really appreciates me. I'm going into Society, I am, through the kindly aid of our friend here, who's taking such a lot of trouble on my account; and you'll find I've got all the qualities to endear me to people who entertain! So now that's all settled, and if you don't mind—I'm an old-fashioned fellow—don't want to turn you out, but—"

"Remember, you'll have to do your proper share of the fighting, dragon!" said St. George, as he took the hint and rose to go. "I mean ramping, and breathing fire, and so on!"

"I can *ramp* all right," replied the dragon, confidently. "As to breathing fire, it's surprising how easily one gets out of practice; but I'll do the best I can. Good-night!"

They had descended the hill and were almost back in the village again, when St. George stopped short. "*Knew* I had forgotten something," he said. "There ought to be a Princess. Terror-stricken and chained to a rock, and all that sort of thing. Boy, can't you arrange a Princess?"

The Boy was in the middle of a tremendous yawn. "I'm tired to death," he wailed, "and I *can't* arrange a Princess, or anything more, at this time of night. And my mother's sitting up, and *do* stop asking me to arrange more things till tomorrow!"

THE CAT WHO BECAME HEAD-FORESTER

A Russian Fairytale

ARTHUR RANSOME

If you drop Vladimir by mistake, you know he always falls on his feet. And if Vladimir tumbles off the roof of the hut, he always falls on his feet. Cats always fall on their feet, on their four paws, and never hurt themselves. And as in tumbling, so it is in life. No cat is ever unfortunate for very long. The worse things look for a cat, the better they are going to be.

Well, once upon a time, not so very long ago, an old peasant had a cat and did not like him. He was a tom-cat, always fighting; and he had lost one ear, and was not very pretty to look at. The peasant thought he would get rid of his old cat, and buy a new one from a neighbour. He did not care what became of the old tom-cat with one ear, so long as he never saw him again. It was no use thinking of killing him, for it is a life's work to kill a cat, and it's likely enough that the cat would come alive at the end.

So the old peasant he took a sack, and he bundled the tom-cat into the sack, and he sewed up the sack and slung it over his back, and walked off into the forest. Off he went, trudging along in the summer sunshine, deep into the forest. And when he had gone very many versts into the forest, he took the sack with the cat in it and threw it away among the trees.

"You stay there," says he, "and if you do get out in this desolate place, much good may it do you, old quarrelsome bundle of bones and fur!"

And with that he turned round and trudged home again, and bought a nice-looking, quiet cat from a neighbour in exchange for a little tobacco, and settled down comfortably at home with the new cat in front of the stove; and there he may be to this day, so far as I know. My story does not bother with him, but only with the old tom-cat tied up in the sack away there out in the forest.

The bag flew through the air, and plumped down through a bush to the ground. And the old tom-cat landed on his feet inside it, very much frightened but not hurt. Thinks he, this bag, this flight through the air, this bump, mean that my life is going to change. Very well; there is nothing like something new now and again.

And presently he began tearing at the bag with his sharp claws. Soon there was a hole he could put a paw through. He went on, tearing and scratching, and there was a hole he could put two paws through. He went on with his work, and soon he could put his head through, all the easier because he had only one ear. A minute or two after that he had wriggled out of the bag, and stood up on his four paws and stretched himself in the forest.

"The world seems to be larger than the village," he said. "I will walk on and see what there is in it."

He washed himself all over, curled his tail proudly up in the air, cocked the only ear he had left, and set off walking under the forest trees.

"I was the head-cat in the village," says he to himself.

"If all goes well, I shall be head here too." And he walked along as if he were the Tzar himself.

Well, he walked on and on, and he came to an old hut that had belonged to a forester. There was nobody there, nor had been for many years, and the old tom-cat made himself quite at home. He climbed up into the loft under the roof, and found a little rotten hay.

"A very good bed," says he, and curls up and falls asleep.

When he woke he felt hungry, so he climbed down and went off in the forest to catch little birds and mice. There were plenty of them in the forest, and when he had eaten enough he came back to the hut, climbed into the loft, and spent the night there very comfortably.

You would have thought he would be content. Not he. He was a cat. He said, "This is a good enough lodging. But I have to catch all my own food. In the village they fed me every day, and I only caught mice for fun. I ought to be able to live like that here. A person of my dignity ought not to have to do all the work for himself."

Next day he went walking in the forest. And as he was walking he met a fox, a vixen, a very pretty young thing, gay and giddy like all girls. And the fox saw the cat, and was very much astonished.

"All these years," she said—for though she was young she thought she had lived a long time—"all these years," she said, "I've lived in the forest, but I've never seen a wild beast like that before. What a strange-looking animal! And with only one ear. How handsome!"

And she came up and made her bows to the cat, and said:

"Tell me, great lord, who you are. What fortunate

chance has brought you to this forest? And by what name am I to call your Excellency?"

Oh! the fox was very polite. It is not every day that you meet a handsome stranger walking in the forest.

The cat arched his back, and set all his fur on end, and said, very slowly and quietly:

"I have been sent from the far forests of Siberia to be Head-forester over you. And my name is Cat Ivanovitch."

"O Cat Ivanovitch!" says the pretty young fox, and she makes more bows. "I did not know. I beg your Excellency's pardon. Will your Excellency honour my humble house by visiting it as a guest?"

"I will," says the cat. "And what do they call you?"

"My name, your Excellency, is Lisabeta Ivanova."

"I will come with you, Lisabeta," says the cat.

And they went together to the fox's earth. Very snug, very neat it was inside; and the cat curled himself up in the best place, while Lisabeta Ivanova, the pretty young fox, made ready a tasty dish of game. And while she was making the meal ready, and dusting the furniture with her tail, she looked at the cat. At last she said, shyly:

"Tell me, Cat Ivanovitch, are your married or single?"

"Single," says the cat.

"And I too am unmarried," says the pretty young fox, and goes busily on with her dusting and cooking.

Presently she looks at the cat again.

"What if we were to marry, Cat Ivanovitch? I would try to be a good wife to you."

"Very well, Lisbeta," says the cat; "I will marry you."

The fox went to her store and took out all the dainties that she had, and made a wedding feast to celebrate her marriage to the great Cat Ivanovitch, who had only one ear, and had come from the far Siberian forests to be Head-forester.

They ate up everything there was in the place.

Next morning the pretty young fox went off busily into the forest to get food for her grand husband. But the old tom-cat stayed at home, and cleaned his whiskers and slept. He was a lazy one, was that cat, and proud.

The fox was running through the forest, looking for game, when she met an old friend, the handsome young wolf, and he began making polite speeches to her.

"What had become of you, gossip?" says he. "I've been to all the best earths and not found you at all."

"Let be, fool," says the fox very shortly. "Don't talk to me like that. What are you jesting about? Formerly I was a young, unmarried fox; now I am a wedded wife."

"Whom have you married, Lisabeta Ivanova?"

"What!" says the fox, "you have not heard that the great Cat Ivanovitch, who has only one ear, has been sent from the far Siberian forests to be Head-forester over all of us? Well, I am now the Head-forester's wife."

"No, I had not heard, Lisabeta Ivanova. And when can I pay my respects to his Excellency?"

"Not now, not now," says the fox. "Cat Ivanovitch will be raging angry with me if I let anyone come near him. Presently he will be taking his food. Look you. Get a sheep, and make it ready, and bring it as a greeting to him, to show him that he is welcome and that you know how to treat him with respect. Leave the sheep near by, and hide yourself so that he shall not see you; for, if he did, things might be awkward."

"Thank you, thank you, Lisabeta Ivanova," says the wolf, and off he goes to look for a sheep.

The pretty young fox went idly on, taking the air, for she knew that the wolf would save her the trouble of looking for food.

Presently she met the bear.

"Good day to you, Lisabeta Ivanova," says the bear; "as pretty as ever, I see you are."

"Bandy-legged one," says the fox; "fool, don't come worrying me. Formerly I was a young, unmarried fox; now I am a wedded wife."

"I beg your pardon," says the bear, "whom have you married, Lisabeta Ivanova?"

"The great Cat Ivanovitch has been sent from the far Siberian forests to be Head-forester over us all. And Cat Ivanovitch is now my husband," says the fox.

"Is it forbidden to have a look at his Excellency?"

"It is forbidden," says the fox. "Cat Ivanovitch will be raging angry with me if I let anyone come near him. Presently he will be taking his food. Get along with you quickly; make ready an ox, and bring it by way of welcome to him. The wolf is bringing a sheep. And look you. Leave the ox near by, and hide yourself so that the great Cat Ivanovitch shall not see you; or else, brother, things may be awkward."

The bear shambled off as fast as he could go to get an ox.

The pretty young fox, enjoying the fresh air of the forests, went slowly home to her earth, and crept in very quietly, so as not to awake the great Head-forester, Cat Ivanovitch, who had only one ear and was sleeping in the best place.

Presently the wolf came through the forest, dragging a sheep he had killed. He did not dare to go too near the fox's earth, because of Cat Ivanovitch, the new Head-forester. So he stopped, well out of sight, and stripped off the skin of the sheep, and arranged the sheep so as to seem a nice tasty morsel. Then he stood still, thinking what to do next. He heard a noise, and looked up. There was the bear, struggling along with a dead ox.

"Good day, brother Michael Ivanovitch," says the wolf.

"Good day, brother Levon Ivanovitch," says the bear. "Have you seen the fox, Lisabeta Ivanova, with her husband, the Head-forester?"

"No, brother," says the wolf. "For a long time I have been waiting to see them."

"Go on and call out to them," says the bear.

"No, Michael Ivanovitch," says the wolf, "I will not

go. Do you go; you are bigger and bolder than I."

"No, no, Levon Ivanovitch, I will not go. There is no use in risking one's life without need."

Suddenly, as they were talking, a little hare came running by. The bear saw him first, and roared out:

"Hi, Squinteye! trot along here."

The hare came up, slowly, two steps at a time, trembling with fright.

"Now then, you squinting rascal," says the bear, "do you know where the fox lives, over there?"

"I know, Michael Ivanovitch."

"Get along there quickly, and tell her that Michael Ivanovitch the bear and his brother Levon Ivanovitch the wolf have been ready for a long time, and have brought presents of a sheep and an ox, as greetings to his Excellency . . ."

"His Excellency, mind," says the wolf; "don't forget."

The hare ran off as hard as he could go, glad to have escaped so easily. Meanwhile the wolf and the bear looked about for good places in which to hide.

"It will be best to climb trees," says the bear. "I shall go up to the top of this fir."

"But what am I to do?" says the wolf. "I can't climb a tree for the life of me. Brother Michael, Brother Michael, hide me somewhere or other before you climb up. I beg you, hide me, or I shall certainly be killed."

"Crouch down under these bushes," says the bear, "and I will cover you with the dead leaves."

"May you be rewarded," says the wolf; and he crouched down under the bushes, and the bear covered him up with dead leaves, so that only the tip of his nose could be seen.

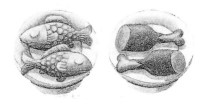

Then the bear climbed slowly up into the fir tree, into the very top, and looked out to see if the fox and Cat Ivanovitch were coming.

They were coming; oh yes, they were coming! The hare ran up and knocked on the door, and said to the fox:

"Michael Ivanovitch the bear and his brother Levon Ivanovitch the wolf have been ready for a long time, and have brought presents of a sheep and an ox as greetings to his Excellency."

"Get along, Squinteye," says the fox; "we are just coming."

And so the fox and the cat set out together.

The bear, up in the top of the tree, saw them, and called down to the wolf:

"They are coming, Brother Levon; they are coming, the fox and her husband. But what a little one he is, to be sure!"

"Quiet, quiet," whispers the wolf. "He'll hear you, and then we are done for."

The cat came up, and arched his back and set all his furs on end, and threw himself on the ox, and began tearing the meat with his teeth and claws. And as he tore he purred. And the bear listened, and heard the purring of the cat, and it seemed to him that the cat was angrily muttering, "Small, small, small . . ."

And the bear whispers: "He's no giant, but what a

glutton! Why, we couldn't get through a quarter of that, and he finds it not enough. Heaven help us if he comes after us!"

The wolf tried to see, but could not, because his head, all but his nose, was covered with the dry leaves. Little by little he moved his head, so as to clear the leaves away from in front of his eyes. Try as he would to be quiet, the leaves rustled, so little, ever so little, but enough to be heard by the one ear of the cat.

The cat stopped tearing the meat and listened.

"I haven't caught a mouse today," he thought.

Once more the leaves rustled.

The cat leapt through the air and dropped with all four paws, and his claws out, on the nose of the wolf. How the wolf yelped! The leaves flew like dust, and the wolf leapt up and ran off as fast as his legs could carry him.

Well, the wolf was frightened, I can tell you, but he was not so frightened as the cat.

When the great wolf leapt up out of the leaves, the cat screamed and ran up the nearest tree, and that was the tree where Michael Ivanovitch the bear was hiding in the topmost branches.

"Oh, he has seen me. Cat Ivanovitch has seen me," thought the bear. He had no time to climb down, and the cat was coming up in long leaps.

The bear trusted to Providence, and jumped from the top of the tree. Many were the branches he broke as he fell; many were the bones he broke when he crashed to the ground. He picked himself up and stumbled off, groaning.

The pretty young fox sat still, and cried out, "Run, run, Brother Levon! . . . Quicker on your pins, Brother

Michael! His Excellency is behind you; his Excellency is close behind!"

Ever since then all the wild beasts have been afraid of the cat, and the cat and the fox live merrily together, and eat fresh meat all the year round, which the other animals kill for them and leave a little way off.

And that is what happened to the old tom-cat with one ear, who was sewn up in a bag and thrown away in the forest.

"Just think what would happen to our handsome Vladimir if we were to throw him away!" said Vanya.

THE MOCK TURTLE'S STORY

In Alice's Adventures in Wonderland, *Alice follows a white rabbit into a hole and finds herself in a magical world where everything is topsy-turvy. After many adventures, she finds herself playing in a curious croquet game led by the Queen of Hearts.*

LEWIS CARROLL

"**Y**ou can't think how glad I am to see you again, you dear old thing!" said the Duchess, as she tucked her arm affectionately into Alice's, and they walked off together.

Alice was very glad to find her in such a pleasant temper, and thought to herself that perhaps it was only the pepper that had made her so savage when they met in the kitchen. "When *I'm* a Duchess," she said to herself (not in a very hopeful tone though), "I won't have any pepper in my kitchen *at all*. Soup does very well without—Maybe it's always pepper that makes people hot-tempered," she went on, very much pleased at having found out a new kind of rule, "and vinegar that makes them sour—and camomile that makes them bitter—and—and barley-sugar and such things that make children sweet-tempered. I only wish people knew *that*: then they wouldn't be so stingy about it, you know—"

She had quite forgotten the Duchess by this time, and was a little startled when she heard her voice close to her ear. "You're thinking about something, my dear, and that makes you forget to talk. I can't tell you just now what the moral of that is, but I shall remember it in a bit."

"Perhaps it hasn't one," Alice ventured to remark.

"Tut, tut, child!" said the Duchess. "Everything's got a moral, if only you can find it." And she squeezed herself up closer to Alice's side as she spoke.

Alice did not much like her keeping so close to her: first, because the Duchess was *very* ugly, and secondly, because she was exactly the right height to rest her chin on Alice's shoulder, and it was an uncomfortably sharp chin. However, she did not like to be rude, so she bore it as well as she could.

"The game's going on rather better now," she said by way of keeping up the conversation a little.

" 'Tis so," said the Duchess: "and the moral of that is—'Oh, 'tis love, 'tis love, that makes the world go round!' "

"Somebody said," Alice whispered, "that it's done by everybody minding their own business!"

"Ah, well! It means much the same thing," said the Duchess, digging her sharp little chin into Alice's shoulder as she added, "and the moral of *that* is—'Take care of the sense, and the sounds will take care of themselves.' "

"How fond she is of finding morals in things!" Alice thought to herself.

"I daresay you're wondering why I don't put my arm round your waist," said the Duchess after a pause: "the reason is, that I'm doubtful about the temper of your flamingo. Shall I try the experiment?"

"He might bite," Alice cautiously replied, not feeling at all anxious to have the experiment tried.

"Very true," said the Duchess: "flamingoes and mustard both bite. And the moral of that is—'Birds of a feather flock together.' "

"Only mustard isn't a bird," Alice remarked.

"Right, as usual," said the Duchess: "what a clear way you have of putting things!"

"It's a mineral, I *think*," said Alice.

"Of course it is," said the Duchess, who seemed ready to agree to everything that Alice said; "there's a large mustard-mine near here. And the moral of that is—'The more there is of mine, the less there is of yours.' "

"Oh, I know!" exclaimed Alice, who had not attended to this last remark, "it's a vegetable. It doesn't look like one, but it is."

"I quite agree with you," said the Duchess, "and the moral of that is—'Be what you would seem to be'—or, if you'd like it put more simply—'Never imagine yourself not to be otherwise than what it might appear to others that what you were or might have been was not otherwise than what you had been would have appeared to them to be otherwise.' "

"I think I should understand that better," Alice said very politely, "if I had it written down: but I can't quite follow it as you say it."

"That's nothing to what I could say if I chose," the Duchess replied in a pleased tone.

"Pray don't trouble yourself to say it any longer than that," said Alice.

"Oh, don't talk about trouble!" said the Duchess. "I make you a present of everything I've said as yet."

"A cheap sort of present!" thought Alice. "I'm glad they don't give birthday presents like that!" But she did not venture to say it out loud.

"Thinking again?" the Duchess asked, with another dig of her sharp little chin.

"I've a right to think," said Alice sharply, for she was beginning to feel a little worried.

"Just about as much right," said the Duchess, "as pigs have to fly: and the m——"

But here, to Alice's great surprise, the Duchess' voice died away, even in the middle of her favourite word "moral," and the arm that was linked into hers began to tremble. Alice looked up, and there stood the Queen in front of them, with her arms folded, frowning like a thunderstorm.

"A fine day, your Majesty!" the Duchess began in a low, weak voice.

"Now, I give you fair warning," shouted the Queen, stamping on the ground as she spoke; "either you or your head must be off, and that in about half no time! Take your choice!"

The Duchess took her choice, and was gone in a moment.

"Let's go on with the game," the Queen said to Alice, and Alice was too much frightened to say a word, but slowly followed her back to the croquet-ground.

The other guests had taken advantage of the Queen's absence, and were resting in the shade: however, the moment they saw her, they hurried back to the game, the Queen merely remarking that a moment's delay would cost them their lives.

All the time they were playing the Queen never left off quarrelling with the other players, and shouting "Off with his head!" or "Off with her head!" Those whom she sentenced were taken into custody by the soldiers, who of course had to leave off being arches to do this, so that by the end of half an hour or so there were no arches

left, and all the players, except the King, the Queen, and Alice, were in custody, and under sentence of execution.

Then the Queen left off, quite out of breath, and said to Alice, "Have you seen the Mock Turtle yet?"

"No," said Alice. "I don't even know what a Mock Turtle is."

"It's the thing Mock Turtle Soup is made from," said the Queen.

"I never saw one, or heard of one," said Alice.

"Come on, then," said the Queen, "and he shall tell you his history."

As they walked off together, Alice heard the King say in a low voice, to the company generally, "You are all pardoned." "Come, *that's* a good thing!" she said to herself, for she had felt quite unhappy at the number of executions the Queen had ordered.

They very soon came upon a Gryphon, lying fast asleep in the sun. (If you don't know what a Gryphon is, look at the picture.) "Up, lazy thing!" said the Queen, "and take this young lady to see the Mock Turtle, and to

hear his history. I must go back and see after some executions I have ordered;" and she walked off, leaving Alice
alone with the Gryphon. Alice did not quite like the look
of the creature, but on the whole she thought it would be
quite as safe to stay with it as to go after that savage Queen:
so she waited.

The Gryphon sat up and rubbed its eyes: then it
watched the Queen till she was out of sight: then it
chuckled. "What fun!" said the Gryphon, half to itself,
half to Alice.

"What *is* the fun?" said Alice.

"Why, *she*," said the Gryphon. "It's all her fancy, that:
they never executes nobody, you know. Come on!"

"Everybody says 'come on!' here," thought Alice, as
she went slowly after it: "I never was so ordered about
before in all my life, never!"

They had not gone far before they saw the Mock
Turtle in the distance, sitting sad and lonely on a little ledge
of rock, and, as they came nearer, Alice could hear him
sighing as if his heart would break. She pitied him deeply.
"What is his sorrow?" she asked the Gryphon, and the
Gryphon answered, very nearly in the same words as
before, "It's all his fancy, that: he hasn't got no sorrow, you
know. Come on!"

So they went up to the Mock Turtle, who looked at
them with large eyes full of tears, but said nothing.

"This here young lady," said the Gryphon, "she
wants for to know your history, she do."

"I'll tell it her," said the Mock Turtle in a deep,
hollow tone: "sit down both of you, and don't speak a
word till I've finished."

So they sat down, and nobody spoke for some

minutes. Alice thought to herself, "I don't see how he can *ever* finish, if he doesn't begin." But she waited patiently.

"Once," said the Mock Turtle at last, with a deep sigh, "I was a real Turtle."

These words were followed by a very long silence, broken only by an occasional exclamation of "Hjckrrh!" from the Gryphon, and the constant heavy sobbing of the Mock Turtle. Alice was very nearly getting up and saying, "Thank you, sir, for your interesting story," but she could not help thinking there *must* be more to come, so she sat still and said nothing.

"When we were little," the Mock Turtle went on at last, more calmly, though still sobbing a little now and then, "we went to school in the sea. The master was an old Turtle—we used to call him Tortoise—"

"Why did you call him Tortoise, if he wasn't one?" Alice asked.

"We called him Tortoise because he taught us," said the Mock Turtle angrily; "really you are very dull!"

"You ought to be ashamed of yourself for asking such a simple question," added the Gryphon; and then they both sat silent and looked at poor Alice, who felt ready to sink into the earth. At last the Gryphon said to the Mock Turtle, "Drive on, old fellow! Don't be all day about it!" and he went on in these words:—

"Yes, we went to school in the sea, though you mayn't believe it—"

"I never said I didn't!" interrupted Alice.

"You did," said the Mock Turtle.

"Hold your tongue!" added the Gryphon, before Alice could speak again. The Mock Turtle went on.

"We had the best of educations—in fact, we went to

school every day—"

"*I've* been to a day-school too," said Alice; "you needn't be so proud as all that."

"With extras?" asked the Mock Turtle a little anxiously.

"Yes," said Alice, "we learned French and music."

"And washing?" said the Mock Turtle.

"Certainly not!" said Alice indignantly.

"Ah! Then yours wasn't a really good school," said the Mock Turtle in a tone of great relief. "Now at *ours* they had at the end of the bill, 'French, music, *and washing*—extra.' "

"You couldn't have wanted it much," said Alice; "living at the bottom of the sea."

"I couldn't afford to learn it," said the Mock Turtle with a sigh. "I only took the regular course."

"What was that?" enquired Alice.

"Reeling and Writhing, of course, to begin with," the Mock Turtle replied: "and then the different branches of Arithmetic—Ambition, Distraction, Uglification, and Derision."

"I never heard of 'Uglification,' " Alice ventured to say. "What is it?"

The Gryphon lifted up both its paws in surprise. "Never heard of uglifying!" it exclaimed. "You know what to beautify is, I suppose?"

"Yes," said Alice, doubtfully: "it means—to—make—anything—prettier."

"Well then," the Gryphon went on, "it you don't know what to uglify is, you *are* a simpleton."

Alice did not feel encouraged to ask any more questions about it, so she turned to the Mock Turtle, and said,

"What else had you to learn?"

"Well, there was Mystery," the Mock Turtle replied, counting off the subjects on his flappers,—"Mystery, ancient and modern, with Seaography: then Drawling—the Drawling-master was an old conger-eel, that used to come once a week: *he* taught us Drawling, Stretching, and Fainting in Coils."

"What was *that* like?" said Alice.

"Well, I can't show it you, myself," the Mock Turtle said: "I'm too stiff. And the Gryphon never learnt it."

"Hadn't time," said the Gryphon: "I went to the Classical master, though. He was an old crab, *he* was."

"I never went to him," the Mock Turtle said with a sigh: "he taught Laughing and Grief, they used to say."

"So he did, so he did," said the Gryphon, sighing in his turn, and both creatures hid their faces in their paws.

"And how many hours a day did you do lessons?" said Alice, in a hurry to change the subject.

"Ten hours the first day," said the Mock Turtle: "nine the next, and so on."

"What a curious plan!" exclaimed Alice.

"That's the reason they're called lessons," the Gryphon remarked: "because they lessen from day to day."

This was quite a new idea to Alice, and she thought it over a little before she made her next remark. "Then the eleventh day must have been a holiday?"

"Of course it was," said the Mock Turtle.

"And how did you manage on the twelfth?" Alice went on eagerly.

"That's enough about lessons," the Gryphon interrupted in a very decided tone: "tell her something about the games now."

THE TWO FROGS

A Japanese Fairytale

ANDREW LANG

Once upon a time in the country of Japan there lived two frogs, one of whom made his home in a ditch near the town of Osaka, on the sea coast, while the other dwelt in a clear little stream which ran through the city of Kioto. At such a great distance apart, they had never even heard of each other; but, funnily enough, the idea came into both their heads at once that they should like to see a little of the world, and the frog who lived at Kioto wanted to visit Osaka, and the frog who lived at Osaka wished to go to Kioto, where the great Mikado had his palace.

So one fine morning in the spring they both set out along the road that led from Kioto to Osaka, one from one end and the other from the other. The journey was more tiring than they expected, for they did not know much about travelling, and half way between the two towns there arose a mountain which had to be climbed. It took them a long time and a great many hops to reach the top, but there they were at last, and what was the surprise of each to see another frog before him! They looked at each other for a moment without speaking, and then fell into conversation, explaining the cause of their meeting so far from their homes. It was delightful to find that they both felt the same wish—to learn a little more of their native country—and as there was no sort of hurry they stretched themselves out in a cool, damp place, and agreed that they would have a good rest before they parted to go their ways.

"What a pity we are not bigger," said the Osaka frog; "for then we could see both towns from here, and tell if it is worth our while going on."

"Oh, that is easily managed," returned the Kioto frog. "We have only got to stand up on our hind legs, and hold on to each other, and then we can each look at the town he is travelling to."

This idea pleased the Osaka frog so much that he at once jumped up and put his front paws on the shoulders of his friend, who had risen also. There they both stood,

stretching themselves as high as they could, and holding each other tightly, so that they might not fall down. The Kioto frog turned his nose towards Osaka, and the Osaka frog turned his nose towards Kioto; but the foolish things forgot that when they stood up their great eyes lay in the backs of their heads, and that though their noses might point to the places to which they wanted to go their eyes beheld the places from which they had come.

"Dear me!" cried the Osaka frog, "Kioto is exactly like Osaka. It is certainly not worth such a long journey. I shall go home!"

"If I had had any idea that Osaka was only a copy of Kioto I should never have travelled all this way," exclaimed the frog from Kioto, and as he spoke he took his hands from his friend's shoulders, and they both fell down on the grass. Then they took a polite farewell of each other, and set off for home again, and to the end of their lives they believed that Osaka and Kioto, which are as different to look at as two towns can be, were as like as two peas.

THE DANCE OF THE ROYAL ANTS

The Little Black Ant *reveals the bustling life and variety of an ant colony through the adventures of one special little black ant.*

ALICE GALL and FLEMING CREW

Birds were singing, bees were humming, and dew-drops sparkled on every bush and tree. Another summer day had come. And inside the mound of sand at the edge of the thicket the ant people were going about their morning tasks.

Little Black Ant liked the early morning hour when the hill began to stir, but this morning there was an unusual thrill about it. This was no ordinary day. Something strange was about to happen.

The halls and corridors were humming with excitement, for news travels swiftly among the ant people, and there was not an ant in all the hill who did not know that today the royal princes and princesses were going away. They were going to leave the hill and go on a mysterious journey. And some of them would never come back.

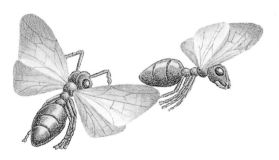

Little Black Ant was thinking about this as she walked along the winding corridor. She had often felt sorry for these royal ants who must stay in their small dark rooms all day long and could not wander through the green grass forest. They were not allowed to do any work at all; no digging, no carrying, no foraging for food. They were not even allowed to help with the cleaning. Little Black Ant did not understand this but she knew it must be right, for it had always been a law among her people that the royal ants should do no work.

And now they were going away! The thought of this made her a little sad. She would miss them, she knew, for they had lived at the hill all their lives and she had seen them almost every day.

"I am glad I am not a royal princess," she said to herself. "I should not like to be going away on a mysterious journey. I should much rather visit the white blossoms where the wells of honey are."

Quickening her pace, she overtook one of the royal princesses. "Good morning, Princess," she said. "You are going away today, aren't you? Won't you tell me about your journey? Where will you go?'

"I do not know," the royal princess said, "but I know that I shall be very merry for this is my wedding day. Did you know that, little Ant?"

"Yes," answered the little ant. "All the hill knows that this is to be a day of weddings for the royal ants."

"It is wonderful," the princess went on eagerly, "for it is said that we will dance all day long in the sunshine, high above the treetops. Just think! I have never used my beautiful wings before, but today I shall fly!"

"Wings are strange things, aren't they?" Little Black Ant said.

"Yes," replied the princess, "and I am glad I have them." She paused for a moment and then added: "I am sorry that you workers have no wings. I wish you were going to fly, too, little Ant."

"Oh, I do not want to fly," Little Black Ant told her. "I would much rather travel on the ground, through the crooked pathways in the grass and among the tangled roots."

They had reached the gateway and the outside world lay before them, sparkling in the sunlight. "Good-bye,

Princess," said Little Black Ant. "I must be off now to look for food."

"Good-bye," replied the princess. "I, too, must be off on my journey high in the air."

"Above the treetops," Little Black Ant said wonderingly.

"Yes, above the treetops," the princess answered. "But I shall not forget you, little Ant, and I shall not forget the good food you so often brought me. Last night it was three drops of honey—the sweetest honey. Do you remember?"

"Yes," said Little Black Ant, "I remember. And now perhaps I shall never bring you honey any more. Perhaps I shall never see you again."

"Who knows?" replied the princess. "Who knows, little Ant?"

There was much more that Little Black Ant would have liked to say, but the sentinel told them to move on so that the other ants could go through the gateway and, without another word, they parted.

The royal princess had seldom before been outside the gates of the hill. Sometimes she had been allowed to walk out here for a little while, accompanied by her attendants; but she had never been free as she was today.

A number of her royal sisters were gathered on the hillside. Some of them had already risen from the ground, their silvery wings glistening as they flew away. The princess moved her own wings restlessly. They felt firm and strong. "They will bear me up," she thought, moving them faster and faster until at last she rose in the air.

She was flying!

Others were flying now, hundreds of them; and, high above the treetops, the royal princesses found their mates as they wheeled and circled in a merry dance. The dance of the royal ants.

But of those who flew that day, few ever found their way back to their home. In this new freedom their wings had given them, most of them flew farther and farther away, letting the breeze carry them where it would.

The royal princess was one of these. She flew high and far. And when evening came she drifted slowly to the ground and found shelter under a blade of grass. The dance was over. Her wings had carried her far from the thicket and her own little mound of sand.

She was alone now. Alone in a strange new world.

TALE OF A TORTOISE AND OF A MISCHIEVOUS MONKEY

A Brazilian Fairytale

ANDREW LANG

Once upon a time there was a country where the rivers were larger, and the forests deeper, than anywhere else. Hardly any men came there, and the wild creatures had it all to themselves, and used to play all sorts of strange games with each other. The great trees, chained one to the other by thick flowering plants with bright scarlet or yellow blossoms, were famous hiding-places for the monkeys, who could wait unseen, till a puma or an elephant passed by, and then jump on their backs and go for a ride, swinging themselves up by the creepers when they had had enough. Near the rivers huge tortoises were to be found, and though to our eyes a tortoise seems a dull, slow thing, it is wonderful to think how clever they were, and how often they outwitted many of their livelier friends.

There was one tortoise in particular that always managed to get the better of everybody, and many were the tales told in the forest of his great deeds. They began when he was quite young, and tired of staying at home with his father and mother. He left them one day, and walked off in search of adventures. In a wide open space surrounded by trees he met with an elephant, who was having his supper before taking his evening bath in the river which ran close by. "Let us see which of us two is strongest," said the young tortoise, marching up to the elephant. "Very well," replied the elephant, much amused at the impertinence of the little creature; "when would you like the trial to be?"

"In an hour's time; I have some business to do first," answered the tortoise. And he hastened away as fast as his short legs would carry him.

In a pool of the river a whale was resting, blowing water into the air and making a lovely fountain. The tortoise, however, was too young and too busy to admire such things, and he called to the whale to stop, as he wanted to speak to him. "Would you like to try which of us is the stronger?" said he. The whale looked at him, sent up another fountain, and answered: "Oh, yes; certainly. When do you wish to begin? I am quite ready."

"Then give me one of your longest bones, and I will fasten it to my leg. When I give the signal, you must pull, and we will see which can pull the hardest."

"Very good," replied the whale; and he took out one of his bones and passed it to the tortoise.

The tortoise picked up the end of the bone in his mouth and went back to the elephant. "I will fasten this to your leg," said he, "in the same way as it is fastened to mine, and we must both pull as hard as we can. We shall soon see which is the stronger." So he wound it carefully round the elephant's leg, and tied it in a firm knot. "Now!" cried he, plunging into a thick bush behind him.

The whale tugged at one end, and the elephant tugged at the other, and neither had any idea that he had not the tortoise for his foe. When the whale pulled hardest

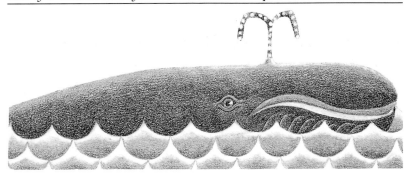

the elephant was dragged into the water; and when the elephant pulled the hardest the whale was hauled on to the land. They were very evenly matched, and the battle was a hard one.

At last they were quite tired, and the tortoise, who was watching, saw that they could play no more. So he crept from his hiding-place, and dipping himself in the river, he went to the elephant and said: "I see that you really are stronger than I thought. Suppose we give it up for to-day?" Then he dried himself on some moss and went to the whale and said: "I see that you really are stronger than I thought. Suppose we give it up for to-day?"

The two adversaries were only too glad to be allowed to rest, and believed to the end of their days that, after all, the tortoise was stronger than either of them.

A day or two later the young tortoise was taking a stroll, when he met a fox, and stopped to speak to him. "Let us try," said he in a careless manner, "which of us can lie buried in the ground during seven years."

"I shall be delighted," answered the fox, "only I would rather that you began."

"It is all the same to me," replied the tortoise; "if you come round this way to-morrow you will see that I have fulfilled my part of the bargain."

So he looked about for a suitable place, and found a convenient hole at the foot of an orange tree. He crept into it, and the next morning the fox heaped up the earth round him, and promised to feed him every day with fresh fruit. The fox so far kept his word that each morning when the sun rose he appeared to ask how the tortoise was getting on. "Oh, very well; but I wish you would give me some fruit," replied he.

"Alas! the fruit is not ripe enough yet for you to eat," answered the fox, who hoped that the tortoise would die of hunger long before the seven years were over.

"Oh dear, oh dear! I am so hungry!" cried the tortoise.

"I am sure you must be; but it will be all right to-morrow," said the fox, trotting off, not knowing that the oranges dropped down the hollow trunk, straight into the tortoise's hole, and that he had as many as he could possibly eat.

So the seven years went by; and when the tortoise came out of his hole he was as fat as ever.

Now it was the fox's turn, and he chose his hole, and the tortoise heaped the earth round, promising to return every day or two with a nice young bird for his dinner. "Well, how are you getting on?" he would ask cheerfully when he paid his visits.

"Oh, all right; only I wish you had brought a bird with you," answered the fox.

"I have been so unlucky, I have never been able to catch one," replied the tortoise. "However, I shall be more fortunate to-morrow, I am sure."

But not many to-morrows after, when the tortoise arrived with his usual question: "Well, how are you getting on?" he received no answer, for the fox was lying in his hole quite still, dead of hunger.

By this time the tortoise was grown up, and was looked up to throughout the forest as a person to be feared for his strength and wisdom. But he was not considered a very swift runner, until an adventure with a deer added to his fame.

One day, when he was basking in the sun, a stag passed by, and stopped for a little conversation. "Would you care to see which of us can run fastest?" asked the tortoise, after some talk. The stag thought the question so silly that he only shrugged his shoulders. "Of course, the victor would have the right to kill the other," went on the tortoise. "Oh, on that condition I agree," answered the deer; "but I am afraid you are a dead man."

"It is no use trying to frighten me," replied the tortoise. "But I should like three days for training; then I shall be ready to start when the sun strikes on the big tree at the edge of the great clearing."

The first thing the tortoise did was to call his brothers and his cousins together, and he posted them carefully under ferns all along the line of the great clearing, making a sort of ladder which stretched for many miles. This done to his satisfaction, he went back to the starting place.

The stag was quite punctual, and as soon as the sun's rays struck the trunk of the tree the stag started off, and was soon far out of the sight of the tortoise. Every now and then he would turn his head as he ran, and call out: "How are you getting on?" and the tortoise who happened to be nearest at that moment would answer: "All right, I am close up to you."

Full of astonishment, the stag would redouble his efforts, but it was no use. Each time he asked: "Are you there?" the answer would come: "Yes, of course, where else should I be?" And the stag ran, and ran, and ran, till he could run no more, and dropped down dead on the grass.

And the tortoise, when he thinks about it, laughs still.

But the tortoise was not the only creature of whose tricks stories were told in the forest. There was a famous monkey who was just as clever and more mischievous, because he was so much quicker on his feet and with his hands. It was quite impossible to catch him and give him the thrashing he so often deserved, for he just swung himself up into a tree and laughed at the angry victim who was sitting below. Sometimes, however, the inhabitants of the forest were so foolish as to provoke him, and then they got the worst of it. This was what happened to the barber, whom the monkey visited one morning, saying that he wished to be shaved. The barber bowed politely to his customer, and begging him to be seated, tied a large cloth round his neck, and rubbed his chin with soap; but instead of cutting off his beard, the barber made a snip at the end of his tail. It was only a very little bit, and the monkey started up more in rage than in pain. "Give me back the end of my tail," he roared, "or I will take one of your razors." The barber refused to give back the missing piece, so the monkey caught up a razor from the table and ran away with it, and no one in the forest could be shaved for days, as there was not another to be got for miles and miles.

As he was making his way to his own particular palm-tree, where the cocoanuts grew, which were so useful for pelting passers-by, he met a woman who was scaling a fish with a bit of wood, for in this side of the forest a few people lived in huts near the river.

"That must be hard work," said the monkey, stopping to look; "try my knife—you will get on quicker." And he handed her the razor as he spoke. A few days later he came back and rapped at the door of the hut. "I have called for my razor," he said, when the woman appeared.

"I have lost it," answered she.

"If you don't give it to me at once I will take your sardine," replied the monkey, who did not believe her. The woman protested she had not got the knife, so he took the sardine and ran off.

A little further along he saw a baker who was standing at the door, eating one of his loaves. "That must be rather dry," said the monkey, "try my fish"; and the man did not need twice telling. A few days later the monkey stopped again at the baker's hut. "I've called for that fish," he said.

"That fish? But I have eaten it!" exclaimed the baker in dismay.

"If you have eaten it I shall take this barrel of meal in exchange," replied the monkey; and he walked off with the barrel under his arm.

As he went he saw a woman with a group of little girls round her, teaching them how to dress hair. "Here is something to make cakes for the children," he said, putting down his barrel, which by this time he found rather heavy. The children were delighted, and ran directly to find some flat stones to bake their cakes on, and when they had made and eaten them, they thought they had never tasted anything so nice. Indeed, when they saw the monkey approaching not long after, they rushed to meet him, hoping that he was bringing them some more presents. But he took no notice of their questions, he only said to their mother: "I've called for my barrel of meal."

"Why, you gave it to me to make cakes of!" cried the mother.

"If I can't get my barrel of meal, I shall take one of your children," answered the monkey. "I am in want of somebody who can bake me bread when I am tired of fruit, and who knows how to make cocoanut cakes."

"Oh, leave me my child, and I will find you another barrel of meal," wept the mother.

"I don't *want* another barrel, I want *that* one," answered the monkey sternly. And as the woman stood wringing her hands, he caught up the little girl that he thought the prettiest and took her to his home in the palm-tree.

She never went back to the hut, but on the whole she was not much to be pitied, for monkeys are nearly as good as children to play with, and they taught her how to swing, and to climb, and to fly from tree to tree, and everything else they knew, which was a great deal.

Now the monkey's tiresome tricks had made him many enemies in the forest, but no one hated him so much as the puma. The cause of their quarrel was known only to themselves, but everybody was aware of the fact, and took care to be out of the way when there was any chance of these two meeting. Often and often the puma had laid traps for the monkey, which he felt sure his foe could not escape; and the monkey would pretend that he saw nothing, and rejoice the hidden puma's heart by seeming to walk straight into the snare, when, lo! a loud laugh would be heard, and the monkey's grinning face would peer out of a mass of creepers and disappear before his foe could reach him.

This state of things had gone on for quite a long while, when at last there came a season such as the oldest parrot in the forest could never remember. Instead of two or three hundred inches of rain falling, which they were all accustomed to, month after month passed without a cloud, and the rivers and springs dried up, till there was only one small pool left for everyone to drink from. There was not an animal for miles round that did not grieve over this shocking condition of affairs, not one at least except the puma. His only thought for years had been how to get the monkey into his power, and this time he imagined his chance had really arrived. He would hide himself in a thicket, and when the monkey came down to drink—and come he must—the puma would spring out and seize him. Yes, on this occasion there could be no escape!

And no more there would have been if the puma had had greater patience; but in his excitement he moved a little too soon. The monkey, who was stooping to drink, heard a rustling, and turning caught the gleam of two yellow, murderous eyes. With a mighty spring he grasped a creeper which was hanging above him, and landed himself on the branch of a tree; feeling the breath of the puma on his feet as the animal bounded from his cover. Never had the monkey been so near death, and it was some time before he recovered enough courage to venture on the ground again.

Up there in the shelter of the trees, he began to turn over in his head plans for escaping the snares of the puma. And at length chance helped him. Peeping down to the earth, he saw a man coming along the path carrying on his head a large gourd filled with honey.

He waited till the man was just underneath the tree, then he hung from a bough, and caught the gourd while the man looked up wondering, for he was no tree-climber. Then the monkey rubbed the honey all over him, and a quantity of leaves from a creeper that was hanging close by; he stuck them all close together into the honey, so that he looked like a walking bush. This finished, he ran to the pool to see the result, and, quite pleased with himself, set out in search of adventures.

Soon the report went through the forest that a new animal had appeared from no one knew where, and that when somebody had asked his name, the strange creature had answered that it was Jack-in-the Green. Thanks to this, the monkey was allowed to drink at the pool as often as he liked, for neither beast nor bird had the faintest notion who he was. And if they made any inquiries the only answer they got was that the water of which he had drunk deeply had turned his hair into leaves, so that they all knew what would happen in case they became too greedy.

By-and-by the great rains began again. The rivers and streams filled up, and there was no need for him to go back to the pool, near the home of his enemy, the puma, as there was a large number of places for him to choose from. So one night, when everything was still and silent, and even the chattering parrots were asleep on one leg, the monkey stole down softly from his perch, and washed off the honey and the leaves, and came out from his bath in his own proper skin. On his way to breakfast he met a rabbit, and stopped for a little talk.

"I am feeling rather dull," he remarked; "I think it would do me good to hunt a while. What do you say?"

"Oh, I am quite willing," answered the rabbit, proud of being spoken to by such a large creature. "But the question is, what shall we hunt?"

"There is no credit in going after an elephant or a tiger," replied the monkey stroking his chin, "they are so big they could not possibly get out of your way. It shows much more skill to be able to catch a small thing that can hide itself in a moment behind a leaf. I'll tell you what! Suppose I hunt butterflies, and you, serpents."

The rabbit, who was young and without experience, was delighted with this idea, and they both set out on their various ways.

The monkey quietly climbed up the nearest tree, and ate fruit most of the day, but the rabbit tired himself to death poking his nose into every heap of dried leaves he saw, hoping to find a serpent among them. Luckily for himself the serpents were all away for the afternoon, at a meeting of their own, for there is nothing a serpent likes so well for dinner as a nice plump rabbit. But, as it was, the dried leaves were all empty, and the rabbit at last fell asleep where he was. Then the monkey, who had been watching him, fell down and pulled his ears, to the rage of the rabbit, who vowed vengeance.

It was not easy to catch the monkey off his guard, and the rabbit waited long before an opportunity arrived. But one day Jack-in-the-Green was sitting on a stone, wondering what he should do next, when the rabbit crept softly behind him, and gave his tail a sharp pull. The monkey gave a shriek of pain, and darted up into a tree, but when he saw that it was only the rabbit who had dared to insult him so, he chattered so fast in his anger, and looked so fierce, that the rabbit fled into the nearest hole, and stayed there for several days, trembling with fright.

Soon after this adventure the monkey went away into another part of the country, right on the outskirt of the forest, where there was a beautiful garden full of oranges hanging ripe from the trees. This garden was a favourite place for birds of all kinds, each hoping to secure an orange for dinner, and in order to frighten the birds away and keep a little fruit for himself, the master had fastened a waxen figure on one of the boughs.

Now the monkey was as fond of oranges as any of the birds, and when he saw a man standing in the tree where the largest and sweetest oranges grew, he spoke to him at once. "You man," he said rudely, "throw me down that big orange up there, or I will throw a stone at you." The wax figure took no notice of this request, so the monkey, who was easily made angry, picked up a stone, and flung it with all his force. But instead of falling to the ground again, the stone stuck to the soft wax.

At this moment a breeze shook the tree, and the orange on which the monkey had set his heart dropped from the bough. He picked it up and ate it every bit, including the rind, and it was so good he thought he should like another. So he called again to the wax figure to throw him an orange, and as the figure did not move, he hurled another stone, which stuck to the wax as the first had done. Seeing that the man was quite indifferent to stones, the monkey grew more angry still, and climbing the tree hastily, gave the figure a violent kick. But like the two stones his leg remained stuck to the wax, and he was held fast. "Let me go at once, or I will give you another kick," he cried, suiting the action to the word, and this time also his foot remained in the grasp of the man. Not knowing what he did, the monkey hit out, first with one hand and then with the other, and when he found that he was literally bound hand and foot, he became so mad with anger and terror that in his struggles he fell to the ground, dragging the figure after him. This freed his hands and feet, but besides the shock of the fall, they had tumbled into a bed of thorns, and he limped away broken and bruised, and groaning loudly; for when monkeys *are* hurt, they take pains that everybody shall know it.

It was a long time before Jack was well enough to go about again; but when he did, he had an encounter with his old enemy the puma. And this was how it came about.

One day the puma invited his friend the stag to go with him and see a comrade, who was famous for the good milk he got from his cows. The stag loved milk, and gladly accepted the invitation, and when the sun began to get a little low the two started on their walk. On the way they arrived on the banks of a river, and as there were no bridges in those days it was necessary to swim across it. The stag was not fond of swimming, and began to say that he was tired, and thought that after all it was not worth going so far to get milk, and that he would return home. But the puma easily saw through these excuses, and laughed at him.

"The river is not deep at all," he said; "why, you will never be off your feet. Come, pluck up your courage and follow me."

The stag was afraid of the river; still, he was much more afraid of being laughed at, and he plunged in after the puma; but in an instant the current had swept him away, and if it had not borne him by accident to a shallow place on the opposite side, where he managed to scramble up the bank, he would certainly have been drowned. As it was, he scrambled out, shaking with terror, and found the puma waiting for him. "You had a narrow escape that time," said the puma.

After resting for a few minutes, to let the stag recover from his fright, they went on their way till they came to a grove of bananas.

"They look very good," observed the puma with a longing glance, "and I am sure you must be hungry, friend stag? Suppose you were to climb the tree and get

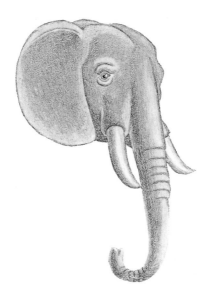

some. You shall eat the green ones, they are the best and sweetest; and you can throw the yellow ones down to me. I dare say they will do quite well?" The stag did as he was bid, though, not being used to climbing, it gave him a deal of trouble and sore knees, and, besides his horns were continually getting entangled in the creepers. What was worse, when once he had tasted the bananas, he found them not at all to his liking, so he threw them all down, green and yellow alike, and let the puma take his choice. And what a dinner he made! When he had *quite* done, they set forth once more.

The path lay through a field of maize, where several men were working. As they came up to them, the puma whispered: "Go on in front, friend stag, and just say 'Bad luck to all workers!' " The stag obeyed, but the men were hot and tired, and did not think this a good joke. So they set their dogs at him, and he was obliged to run away as fast as he could.

"I hope your industry will be rewarded as it deserves," said the puma as he passed along; and the men were pleased, and offered him some of their maize to eat.

By-and-by the puma saw a small snake with a beautiful shining skin, lying coiled up at the foot of a tree. "What a lovely bracelet that would make for your daughter, friend stag!" said he. The stag stooped and picked up the snake, which bit him, and he turned angrily to the puma. "Why did you not tell me it would bite?" he asked.

"Is it my fault if you are an idiot?" replied the puma.

At last they reached their journey's end, but by this time it was late, and the puma's comrade was ready for bed, so they slung their hammocks in convenient places, and went to sleep. But in the middle of the night the puma rose softly and stole out of the door to the sheep-fold, where he killed and ate the fattest sheep he could find, and taking a bowl full of its blood, he sprinkled the sleeping stag with it. This done, he returned to bed.

In the morning the shepherd went as usual to let the sheep out of the fold, and found one of them missing. He thought directly of the puma, and ran to accuse him of having eaten the sheep. "I, my good man? What has put it into your head to think of such a thing? Have *I* got any blood about me? If anyone has eaten a sheep it must be my friend the stag." Then the shepherd went to examine the sleeping stag, and of course he saw the blood. "Ah! I will teach you how to steal!" cried he, and he hit the stag such a blow on his skull that he died in a moment. The noise awakened the comrade above, and he came downstairs. The puma greeted him with joy, and begged he might have some of the famous milk as soon as possible, for he was very thirsty. A large bucket was set before the puma directly. He drank it to the last drop, and then took leave.

On his way home he met the monkey. "Are you fond of milk?" asked he. "I know a place where you get it very nice. I will show you it if you like." The monkey knew that the puma was not so good-natured for nothing, but he felt quite able to take care of himself, so he said he should have much pleasure in accompanying his friend.

They soon reached the same river, and, as before, the puma remarked: "Friend monkey, you will find it very shallow; there is no cause for fear. Jump in, and I will follow."

"Do you think you have the stag to deal with?" asked the monkey, laughing. "I should prefer to follow; if not I shall go no further." The puma understood that it was useless trying to make the monkey do as he wished, so he chose a shallow place and began to swim across. The monkey waited till the puma had got to the middle, then he gave a great spring and jumped on his back, knowing quite well that the puma would be afraid to shake him off, lest he should be swept away into deep water. So in this manner they reached the bank.

The banana grove was not far distant, and here the puma thought he would pay the monkey out for forcing him to carry him over the river. "Friend monkey, look what fine bananas," cried he. "You are fond of climbing; suppose you run up and throw me down a few. You can eat the green ones, which are the nicest, and I will be content with the yellow."

"Very well," answered the monkey, swinging himself up; but he ate all the yellow ones himself, and only threw down the green ones that were left. The puma was furious and cried out: "I will punch your head for that." But the monkey only answered: "If you are going to talk such nonsense I won't walk with you." And the puma was silent.

In a few minutes more they arrived at the field where the man were reaping the maize, and the puma remarked as he had done before: "Friend monkey, if you wish to please these men, just say as you go by: 'Bad luck to all workers.' "

"Very well," replied the monkey; but, instead, he nodded and smiled, and said: "I hope your industry may be rewarded as it deserves." The men thanked him heartily, let him pass on, and the puma followed behind him.

Further along the path they saw the shining snake lying on the moss. "What a lovely necklace for your daughter," exclaimed the puma. "Pick it up and take it with you."

"You are very kind, but I will leave it for you," answered the monkey, and nothing more was said about the snake.

Not long after this they reached the comrade's house, and found him just ready to go to bed. So, without stopping to talk, the guests slung their hammocks, the monkey taking care to place his so high that no one could get at him. Besides, he thought it would be more prudent not to fall asleep, so he only lay still and snored loudly. When it was quite dark and no sound was to be heard, the puma crept out to the sheep-fold, killed the sheep, and carried back a bowl full of its blood with which to sprinkle the monkey. But the monkey, who had been watching him out of the corner of his eye, waited until the puma drew near, and with a violent kick upset the bowl all over the puma himself.

When the puma saw what had happened, he turned in a great hurry to leave the house, but before he could do so, he saw the shepherd coming, and hastily lay down again.

"This is the second time I have lost a sheep," the man said to the monkey; "it will be the worse for the thief when I catch him, I can tell you." The monkey did not answer, but silently pointed to the puma who was pretending to be asleep. The shepherd stooped and saw the blood, and cried out: "Ah! so it is you, is it? Then take that!" and with his stick he gave the puma such a blow on the head that he died then and there.

Then the monkey got up and went to the dairy, and drank all the milk he could find. Afterwards he returned home and married, and that is the last we heard of him.

THE ENCHANTED HORSE

ANDREW LANG

It was the Feast of the New Year, the oldest and most splendid of all the feasts in the Kingdom of Persia, and the day had been spent by the king in the city of Schiraz, taking part in the magnificent spectacles prepared by his subjects to do honour to the festival. The sun was setting, and the monarch was about to give his court the signal to retire when suddenly an Indian appeared before his throne, leading a horse richly harnessed, and looking in every respect exactly like a real one.

"Sire," said he, prostrating himself as he spoke, "although I make my appearance so late before Your Highness, I can confidently assure you that none of the wonders you have seen during the day can be compared to this horse, if you will deign to cast your eyes upon him."

"I see nothing in it," replied the king, "except a clever imitation of a real horse; any skilled workman might do as much."

"Sire," returned the Indian, "it is not of his outward form that I would speak but of the use I can make of him. I have only to mount him and wish myself in some special place and, no matter how distant it may be, in a very few moments I shall find myself there. It is this, sire, that makes the horse so marvellous, and if Your Highness will allow me, you can prove it for yourself."

The King of Persia, who was interested in everything out of the common and had never before come across a horse with such qualities, bade the Indian mount the animal and show what he could do. In an instant the man had vaulted on his back and inquired where the monarch wished to send him.

"Do you see that mountain?" asked the king, pointing to a huge mass that towered into the sky about three leagues from Schiraz. "Go and bring me the leaf of a palm that grows at the foot."

The words were hardly out of the king's mouth when the Indian turned a screw placed in the horse's neck close to the saddle, and the animal bounded like lightning up into the air and was soon beyond the sight even of the sharpest eyes. In a quarter of an hour the Indian was seen returning, bearing in his hand the palm. Guiding his horse to the foot of the throne, he dismounted and laid the leaf before the king.

Now the monarch had no sooner proved the astounding speed of which the horse was capable than he longed to possess it himself. Indeed, so sure was he that the Indian would be quite ready to sell it, he looked upon it as his own already.

"I never guessed from his mere outside how valuable an animal he was," he remarked to the Indian, "and I am grateful to you for having shown me my error. If you will sell it, name your own price."

"Sire," replied the Indian, "I never doubted that a sovereign so wise and accomplished as Your Highness would do justice to my horse, when he once knew its power; I even went so far as to think it probable that you might wish to possess it. Greatly as I prize it, I will yield it up to Your Highness on one condition. The horse was not constructed by me, but it was given me by the inventor in exchange for my only daughter, who made me take a solemn oath that I would never part with it, except for some object of equal value."

"Name anything you like," cried the monarch, interrupting him. "My kingdom is large and filled with fair cities. You have only to choose which you would prefer, to become its ruler to the end of your life."

"Sire," answered the Indian, to whom the proposal did not seem nearly so generous as it appeared to the king, "I am most grateful to Your Highness for your princely offer and beseech you not to be offended with me if I say I can only deliver up my horse in exchange for the hand of the princess, your daughter."

A shout of laughter burst from the courtiers as they heard these words, and Prince Firouz Schah, the heir apparent, was filled with anger at the Indian's presumption. The king, however, thought that it would not cost him much to part from the princess in order to gain such a delightful toy and while he was hesitating as to his answer the prince broke in.

"Sire," he said, "it is not possible that you can doubt for an instant what reply you should give to such insolence. Consider what you owe to yourself and to the blood of your ancestors.

"My son," replied the king, "you speak nobly, but you do not realize either the value of the horse, or the fact that if I reject the proposal of the Indian he will only make the same to some other monarch, and I should be filled with despair at the thought that anyone but myself should own this seventh wonder of the world. Of course I do not say that I shall accept his conditions, and perhaps he may be brought to reason. Meanwhile I should like you to examine the horse and, with the owner's permission, to make trial of its powers."

The Indian, who had overhead the king's speech, thought that he saw in it signs of yielding to his proposal, so he joyfully agreed to the monarch's wishes. He came forward to help the prince mount the horse and show him how to guide it. But, before he had finished, the young man turned the screw and was soon out of sight.

They waited some time, expecting that every moment the prince might be seen returning in the distance, but at length the Indian grew frightened. Prostrating himself before the throne, he said to the king, "Sire, Your Highness must have noticed that the prince, in his impatience, did not allow me to tell him what it was necessary to do in order to return to the place from which he started. I implore you not to punish me for what was not my fault and not to blame me for any misfortune that may occur."

"But why," cried the king in a burst of fear and anger, "why did you not call him back when you saw him disappearing?"

"Sire," replied the Indian, "the rapidity of his movements took me so by surprise that he was out of hearing before I recovered my speech. But we must hope that he will perceive and turn a second screw, which will have the effect of bringing the horse back to earth."

"But supposing he does," answered the king, "what

is to hinder the horse from descending straight into the sea or dashing him to pieces on the rocks!"

"Have no fears, Your Highness," said the Indian; "the horse has the gift of passing over seas and of carrying his rider wherever he wishes to go."

"Well, your head shall answer for it," returned the monarch, "if in three months he is not safe back with me or at any rate does not send me news of his safety, your life shall pay the penalty." So saying, he ordered his guards to seize the Indian and throw him into prison.

Meanwhile, Prince Firouz Schah had gone gaily up into the air and for the space of an hour continued to ascend higher and higher, till the very mountains were not distinguishable from the plains. Then he began to think it was time to come down and took for granted that, in order to do this, it was only needful to turn the screw the reverse way; but to his surprise and horror he found that, turn as he might, he did not make the smallest impression. He then remembered that he had never waited to ask how he was to get back to earth again and understood the danger in which he stood. Luckily, he did not lose his head, and set about examining the horse's neck with great care; at last, to his intense joy, he discovered a tiny little peg, much smaller than the other, close to the right ear. This he turned and found himself dropping to the earth, though more slowly than he had left it.

It was now dark and, as the prince could see nothing, he was obliged, not without some feeling of disquiet, to allow the horse to direct his own course. Midnight was already passed before Prince Firouz Schah again touched the ground, faint and weary from his long ride and from the fact that he had eaten nothing since early morning.

The first thing he did on dismounting was to try to find out where he was, and as far as he could discover in the thick darkness, he found himself on the terraced roof of a huge palace, with a balustrade of marble running round it. In one corner of the terrace stood a small door, opening on to a staircase which led down into the palace.

Some people might have hesitated before exploring further, but not so the prince. "I am doing no harm," he said, "and whoever the owner may be, he will not touch me when he sees I am unarmed," and in dread of making a false step, he went cautiously down the staircase. On a landing he noticed an open door, beyond which was a faintly lighted hall.

Before entering, the prince paused and listened, but he heard nothing except the sound of men snoring. By the light of a lantern suspended from the roof, he perceived a row of black guards sleeping, each with a naked sword lying by him, and he understood that the hall must form the anteroom to the chamber of some queen or princess.

Standing quite still, Prince Firouz Schah looked about him till his eyes grew accustomed to the gloom and he noticed a bright light shining through a curtain in one corner. He then made his way softly toward it and, drawing aside its folds, passed into a magnificent chamber full of sleeping women, all lying on low couches, except one who was on a sofa. This one, he knew, must be the princess.

Gently stealing up to the side of her bed he looked at her and saw that she was more beautiful than any woman he had ever beheld. But, fascinated though he was, he was well aware of the danger of his position, as one cry of sur-prise would awake the guards and cause his certain death.

So sinking quietly on his knees, he took hold of the

princess's sleeve and drew her arm lightly toward him. The princess opened her eyes, and seeing before her a handsome well-dressed man, she remained speechless with astonishment.

This favourable moment was seized by the prince who, bowing low while he knelt, thus addressed her, "You behold, madam, a prince in distress, son to the King of Persia, who, owing to an adventure so strange that you will scarcely believe it, finds himself here, a suppliant for your protection. But yesterday, I was in my father's court, engaged in the celebration of our most solemn festival; today, I am in an unknown land in danger of my life."

Now the princess, whose mercy Prince Firouz Schah implored, was the eldest daughter of the King of Bengal, and was enjoying rest and change in the palace her father had built her at a little distance from the capital.

She listened kindly to what Firouz Schah had to say, and then answered, "Prince, be not uneasy; hospitality and humanity are practised as widely in Bengal as they are in Persia. The protection you ask will be given you by all. You have my word for it." As the prince was about to thank her, she added quickly, "However great may be my curiosity to learn by what means you have travelled here so speedily, I know that you must be faint for want of food, so I shall give orders to my women to take you to one of my chambers, where you will be provided with supper and left to repose."

By this time the princess's attendants were all awake and listening to the conversation. At a sign from their mistress they rose, dressed themselves hastily, and snatching up some tapers which lighted the room, conducted the prince to a large and lofty room, where two of the number prepared his bed and the rest went down to the kitchen from which they soon returned with all sorts of dishes. Then, showing him cupboards filled with dresses and linen, they quitted the room.

During their absence the Princess of Bengal, who had been greatly struck by the beauty of the prince, tried in vain to go to sleep again. It was of no use; she felt wide awake and when her women entered the room she inquired eagerly if the prince had all he wanted and what they thought of him.

"Madam," they replied, "it is of course impossible for us to tell what impression this young man has made on you. For ourselves, we think you would be fortunate if the king your father should allow you to marry anyone so amiable. Certainly there is no one in the Court of Bengal who can be compared with him."

These flattering observations were by no means displeasing to the princess but, as she did not wish to betray her own feelings, she merely said, "You are all a set of chatterboxes; go back to bed and let me sleep."

When she dressed the following morning her maids noticed that, contrary to her usual habit, the princess was very particular about her toilette and insisted on her hair being dressed two or three times over. "For," she said to herself, "if my appearance was not displeasing to the prince when he saw me in the condition I was, how much more will he be struck with me when he beholds me with all my charms."

Then she placed in her hair the largest and most brilliant diamonds she could find and arrayed herself with a necklace, bracelets and girdle, all of precious stones. And over her shoulders her ladies put a robe of the richest stuff in all the Indies that no one was allowed to wear except members of the royal family. When she was fully dressed according to her wishes, she sent to know if the Prince of Persia was awake and ready to receive her, as she desired to present herself before him.

When the princess's messenger entered his room Prince Firouz Schah was in the act of leaving it, to inquire if he might be allowed to pay his homage to her mistress. On hearing the princess's wishes, he at once gave way. "Her will is my law," he said, "I am only here to obey her orders."

In a few moments the princess herself appeared and, after the usual compliments had passed between them, the princess sat down on a sofa and began to explain to the prince her reasons for not giving him an audience in her own apartments. "Had I done so," she said, "we might

have been interrupted at any hour by the chief of the eunuchs, who has the right to enter whenever it pleases him, whereas this is forbidden ground. I am all impatience to learn the wonderful accident which has procured the pleasure of your arrival and that is why I have come to you here, where no one can intrude upon us. Begin then, I entreat you, without delay."

So the prince began at the beginning and told all the story of the festival of Nedrouz held yearly in Persia and of the splendid spectacles celebrated in its honour. But when he came to the enchanted horse, the princess declared that she could never have imagined anything half so surprising. "Well then," continued the prince, "you can easily understand how the king, my father, who has a passion for all curious things, was seized with a violent desire to possess this horse and asked the Indian what sum he would take for it.

"The man's answer was absolutely absurd, as you will agree, when I tell you that it was nothing less than the hand of the princess, my sister. But though all the bystanders laughed and mocked and I was beside myself with rage, I saw to my despair that my father could not make up his mind to treat the insolent proposal as it deserved. I tried to argue with him but in vain. He only begged me to examine the horse with a view, as I quite understood, of making me more sensible of its value.

"To please my father, I mounted the horse and, without waiting for any instructions from the Indian, turned the peg as I had seen him do. In an instant I was soaring upward, much quicker than an arrow could fly, and felt as if I must be getting so near the sky that I should soon hit my head against it! I could see nothing beneath me and for some time was so confused I did not even know in what direction I was travelling. At last, when it was growing dark, I found another screw; on turning it, the horse began slowly to sink toward the earth. I was forced to trust to chance and to see what fate had in store, and it was already past midnight when I found myself on the roof of this palace. I crept down the little staircase and made directly for a light which I perceived through an open door. I peeped cautiously in and saw, as you will guess, the eunuchs lying asleep on the floor. I knew the risks I ran but my need was so great I paid no attention to them and stole safely past your guards to the curtain which concealed your doorway.

"The rest, Princess, you know. It only remains for me to thank you for the kindness you have shown me and to assure you of my gratitude. By the law of nations I am already your slave, and I have only my heart that is my own to offer you. But what am I saying? My own? Alas, madam, it was yours from the moment I first beheld you!"

The air with which he said these words could have left no doubt in the mind of the princess as to the effect of her charms, and the blush which mounted to her face only increased her beauty.

"Prince," returned she, as soon as her confusion permitted her to speak, "you have given me the greatest pleasure, and I have followed you closely in all your adventures. Though you are positively sitting before me, I even trembled at your danger in the upper regions of the air! Let me say what a debt I owe to the chance which led you to my house; you could have entered none which would have given you a warmer welcome. As to your being a slave, of course that is merely a joke, and my reception must itself have assured you that you are as free here as at your father's court.

"As to your heart," continued she in tones of encouragement, "I am quite sure that must have been disposed of long ago to some princess who is well worthy of it, and I could not think of being the cause of your unfaithfulness to her."

Prince Firouz Schah was about to protest there was no lady with prior claims, but he was stopped by the entrance of one of the princess's attendants, who announced that dinner was served and neither was sorry for the interruption.

Dinner was laid in a magnificent apartment, the table was covered with delicious fruits, and during the repast richly dressed girls sang softly and sweetly to stringed instruments. After the prince and princess had dined, they passed into a small room hung with blue and gold, looking out into a garden stocked with flowers and trees, quite different from any that were to be found in Persia.

"Princess," observed the young man, "till now I had always believed that Persia could boast finer palaces and more lovely gardens than any kingdom upon earth. But my eyes have been opened, and I begin to perceive that wherever there is a great king he will surround himself with buildings worthy of him."

"Prince," replied the Princess of Bengal, "I have no idea what a Persian palace is like, so I am unable to make comparisons. I do not wish to depreciate my own palace but I can assure you it is very poor beside that of the king, my father, as you will agree when you have been there to greet him, which I hope you will shortly do."

Now the princess hoped that by bringing about a

meeting between the prince and her father, the king would be so struck with the young man's distinguished air and fine manners he would offer him his daughter to wife. But the reply of the Prince of Persia to her suggestion was not quite what she wished.

"Madam," he said, "by taking advantage of your proposal to visit the palace of the King of Bengal, I should satisfy not merely my curiosity, but also the sentiments of respect with which I regard him. But, Princess, I am persuaded you will feel with me that I cannot possibly present myself before so great a sovereign without the attendants suitable to my rank. He would think me an adventurer."

"If that is all," she answered, "you can get as many attendants here as you please. There are plenty of Persian merchants and, as for money, my treasury is always open to you. Take what you please."

Prince Firouz Schah guessed what prompted so much kindness on the part of the princess and was much touched by it. Still his passion, which increased every moment, did not make him forget his duty.

So he replied without hesitation, "I do not know, Princess, how to express my gratitude for your obliging offer, which I would accept at once if it were not for the recollection of all the uneasiness the king, my father, must be suffering on my account. I should be unworthy indeed of all the love he showers upon me, if I did not return to him at the first possible moment. For, while I am enjoying the society of the most amiable of all princesses, he is, I am quite convinced, plunged in the deepest grief, having lost all hope of seeing me again. I am sure you will understand my position and will feel that to remain away one instant longer than is necessary would not only be ungrateful on my part but perhaps even a crime, for how do I know if my absence may not break his heart?

"But," continued the prince, "having obeyed the voice of my conscience, I shall count the moments when, with your gracious permission, I may present myself before the King of Bengal, not as a wanderer but as a prince, to implore the favour of your hand. My father has always informed me that in my marriage I shall be left quite free, but I am persuaded that I have only to describe your generosity for my wishes to become his own."

The Princess of Bengal was too reasonable not to accept the explanation offered by Prince Firouz Schah, but she was much disturbed at his intention of departing at once, for she feared that, no sooner had he left her, the impression she had made on him would fade away. So she made one more effort to keep him and, after assuring him that she entirely approved of his anxiety to see his father, begged him to give her a day or two more of his company.

In common politeness the prince could hardly refuse this request, and the princess set about inventing every kind of amusement for him and succeeded so well that two months slipped by almost unnoticed, in balls, spectacles and in hunting, of which, when unattended by danger, the princess was passionately fond. But at last, one day, the prince declared seriously he could neglect his duty no longer and entreated her to put no further obstacles in his way, promising at the same time to return as soon as he could, with all the magnificence due both to her and to himself.

"Princess," he added, "it may be that in your heart you class me with those false lovers whose devotion cannot stand the test of absence. If you do, you wrong me.

Were it not for fear of offending you, I would beseech you to come with me, for my life can only be happy when passed with you. As for your reception at the Persian Court, it will be as warm as your merits deserve and as for what concerns the King of Bengal, he must be much more indifferent to your welfare than you have led me to believe if he does not give his consent to our marriage."

The princess could not find words in which to reply to the arguments of the Prince of Persia, but her silence and her downcast eyes spoke for her and declared that she had no objection to accompanying him on his travels. The only difficulty that occurred to her was that Prince Firouz Schah did not know how to manage the horse, and she dreaded lest they might find themselves in the same plight as before. But the prince soothed her fears so successfully, she soon had no other thought than to arrange for their flight so secretly that no one in the palace should suspect it.

This was done, and early the following morning, when the whole palace was wrapped in sleep, she stole up on to the roof where the prince was already awaiting her, with his horse's head towards Persia. He mounted first and helped the princess up behind. Then, when she was firmly seated, with her hands holding tightly to his belt, he touched the screw and the horse began to leave the earth quickly behind him.

He travelled with his accustomed speed, and Prince Firouz Schah guided him so well that in two hours and a half from the time of starting he saw the capital of Persia lying beneath him. He determined to alight neither in the great square from which he had started, nor in the sultan's palace, but at a country house a little distance from the town. Here he showed the princess a beautiful suite of rooms and begged her to rest, while he informed his father of their arrival and prepared a public reception worthy of her rank. Then he ordered a horse to be saddled and set out.

All the way through the streets he was welcomed with shouts of joy by the people, who had long lost all hope of seeing him again. On reaching the palace he found the sultan surrounded by his ministers, all clad in the deepest mourning, and his father almost went out of his mind with surprise and delight at the mere sound of his son's voice. When he had calmed down a little he begged the prince to relate his adventures.

The prince at once seized the opening thus given him and told the whole story of his treatment by the Princess of Bengal, not even concealing the fact that she had fallen in love with him. "And, sire," he added, "having given my royal word that you would not refuse your consent to our marriage, I persuaded her to return with me on the Indian's horse. I have left her in one of Your Highness" country houses, where she is waiting anxiously to be assured that I have not promised in vain."

As he said this the prince was about to throw himself at the feet of the sultan, but his father prevented him, and embracing him again, said eagerly, "My son, not only do I gladly consent to your marriage with the Princess of Bengal, but I will hasten to pay my respects to her and thank her in my own person for the benefits she has conferred on you. I will then bring her back with me and make all arrangements for the wedding to be celebrated today."

So the sultan gave orders that the mourning worn by the people should be thrown off and there should be a concert of drums, trumpets and cymbals. Also that the Indian should be taken from prison and brought before him.

His commands were obeyed, and the Indian was led into his presence, surrounded by guards. "I have kept you locked up," said the sultan, "in case my son was lost, that your life should pay the penalty. He has now returned, so take your horse and begone for ever."

The Indian hastily quitted the presence of the sultan, and when he was outside he inquired of the man who had taken him out of prison where the prince had really been all this time, and what he had been doing. They told him the whole story and how the Princess of Bengal was even then awaiting in the country palace the consent of the sultan, which at once put into the Indian's head a plan of revenge for the treatment he had received. Going straight to the country house, he informed the doorkeeper who was left in charge that he had been sent by the sultan and by the Prince of Persia to bring the princess and the enchanted horse to the palace.

The doorkeeper knew the Indian by sight and was of course aware that nearly three months before he had been thrown into prison by the sultan. Seeing him at liberty, the man took for granted that he was speaking the truth and made no difficulty about leading him before the Princess of Bengal; while on her side, hearing that he had come from the prince, the lady gladly consented to do what he wished.

The Indian, delighted with the success of his scheme, mounted the horse, assisted the princess to mount behind him, and turned the peg at the very moment the prince was leaving the palace in Schiraz for the country house, followed closely by the sultan and all the court. Knowing this, the Indian deliberately steered the horse right above the city, in order that his revenge for his unjust imprisonment might be all the quicker and sweeter.

When the Sultan of Persia saw the horse and its riders, he stopped short in astonishment and horror and broke out into oaths, which the Indian heard quite unmoved, knowing that he was perfectly safe from pursuit. But mortified and furious as the sultan was, his feelings were nothing to those of Prince Firouz Schah on seeing the object of his passionate devotion being borne rapidly away. And while he was struck speechless with grief and remorse at not having guarded her better, she vanished swiftly out of his sight. What was he to do? Should he follow his father into the palace and there give up to his despair? Both his love and his courage forbade it; and he continued his way to the country house.

The sight of the prince showed the doorkeeper of what folly he had been guilty and, flinging himself at his master's feet, he implored his pardon. "Rise," said the prince, "I am the cause of this misfortune, not you. Go and find me the dress of a dervish but beware of saying it is for me."

At a short distance from the country house a convent of dervishes was situated, and the superior, or scheik, was the doorkeeper's friend. So it was easy enough to obtain a dervish's dress, which the prince at once put on instead of his own. Disguised like this and concealing about him a box of pearls and diamonds he had intended as a present to the princess, he left the house at nightfall, uncertain where he should go but firmly resolved not to return without her.

Meanwhile the Indian had turned the horse in such direction that, before many hours had passed, it had entered a wood close to the capital of the kingdom of Cashmere. Feeling very hungry and supposing that the princess also might be in want of food, he brought his steed down to the earth and left the princess in a shady place on the banks of a clear stream.

At first, when the princess found herself alone, the idea occurred to her of trying to escape and hide herself. But as she had eaten scarcely anything since she had left Bengal, she felt too weak to venture far and was obliged to abandon her design. On the return of the Indian with meats of various kinds she began to eat voraciously and soon had regained sufficient courage to reply with spirit to his insolent remarks. Goaded by his threats she sprang to her feet, calling loudly for help, and luckily her cries were heard by a troop of horsemen, who rode up to inquire what was the matter.

Now the leader of these horsemen was the Sultan of Cashmere, returning from the chase, and he instantly turned to the Indian to inquire who he was and who the lady was he had with him. The Indian rudely answered that it was his wife and there was no occasion for anyone else to interfere between them.

The princess who, of course, was ignorant of the rank of her deliverer, denied altogether the Indian's story. "My lord," she cried, "whoever you may be, put no faith in this impostor. He is an abominable magician, who has this day torn me from the Prince of Persia, my destined husband, and has brought me here on this enchanted horse." She would have continued but her tears choked her, and the Sultan of Cashmere, convinced by her beauty and her distinguished air, of the truth of her tale, ordered his followers to cut off the Indian's head, which was done immediately.

But rescued though she was from one peril, it seemed as if she had only fallen into another. The sultan commanded a horse to be given her and conducted her to his own palace, where he led her to a beautiful apartment, selected female slaves to wait on her and eunuchs to be her guard. Then, without allowing her time to thank him for all he had done, he bade her repose, saying she should tell him her adventures on the following day.

The princess fell asleep, flattering herself that she had only to relate her story for the sultan to be touched by compassion and restore her to the prince without delay. But a few hours were to undeceive her.

When the Sultan of Cashmere had quitted her presence the evening before, he resolved that the sun should not set again without the princess becoming his wife. At daybreak, proclamation of his intention was made throughout the town by the sound of drums, trumpets, cymbals and other instruments calculated to fill the heart with joy. The Princess of Bengal was early awakened by the noise, but she did not for one moment imagine it had anything to do with her, till the sultan, arriving as soon as she was dressed to inquire after her health, informed her that the trumpet blasts she heard were part of the solemn marriage ceremonies, for which he begged her to prepare. This unexpected announcement caused the princess such terror that she sank down in a dead faint.

The slaves that were in waiting ran to her aid, and the sultan himself did his best to bring her back to consciousness, but for a long while it was all to no purpose. At length her senses began slowly to come back to her and then, rather than break faith with the Prince of Persia by consenting to such a marriage, she determined to feign madness. So she began by saying all sorts of absurdities and using all kinds of strange gestures, while the sultan stood watching her with sorrow and surprise. But as this sudden seizure showed no signs of abating, he left her to her women, ordering them to take the greatest care of her. Still, as the day went on, the malady seemed to become worse and by night it was almost violent.

Days passed in this manner, till at last the sultan decided to summon all the doctors of his court to consult together over her sad state. Their answer was that madness is of so many different kinds it was impossible to give an opinion on the case without seeing the princess, so the sultan gave orders they were to be introduced into her chamber, one by one, every man according to his rank.

This decision had been foreseen by the princess, who knew quite well that once she allowed the physicians to feel her pulse the most ignorant of them would discover that she was in perfectly good health and her madness was feigned, so as each man approached she broke out into such violent paroxysms that not one dared to lay a finger on her. A few, who pretended to be cleverer than the rest, declared they could diagnose sick people without seeing them and ordered her certain potions, which she made no difficulty about taking as she was persuaded they were all harmless.

When the Sultan of Cashmere saw that the court doctors could do nothing toward curing the princess, he called in those of the city, who fared no better. Then he had recourse to the most celebrated physicians in the other large towns but, finding the task was beyond their science, he finally sent messengers into the other neighbouring states, with a memorandum containing full particulars of the princess's madness, offering at the same time to pay the expenses of any physician who would come and see for himself, and a handsome reward to the one who should cure her. In answer to this proclamation many foreign professors flocked into Cashmere, but they naturally were not more successful than the rest had been as the cure depended neither on them, nor their skill, but only on the princess herself.

It was during this time that Prince Firouz Schah, wandering sadly and hopelessly from place to place, arrived in a large city of India, where he heard a great deal of talk about the Princess of Bengal who had gone out of her senses on the very day that she was to have been married to the Sultan of Cashmere. This was quite enough to induce him to take the road to Cashmere and to inquire the full particulars of the story at the first inn at which he lodged in the capital. When he knew that he had at last found the princess whom he had so long lost, he set about devising a plan for her rescue.

The first thing he did was to procure a doctor's robe, that his dress, added to the long beard he had allowed to grow on his travels, might unmistakably proclaim his profession. He then lost no time in going to the palace, where he obtained an audience of the chief usher and while apologizing for his boldness in presuming to think he could cure the princess, where so many others had failed, declared he had the secret of certain remedies which had hitherto never failed of their effect.

The chief usher assured him that he was heartily welcome and the sultan would receive him with pleasure; and in case of success, he would gain a magnificent reward.

When the Prince of Persia, in the disguise of a physician, was brought before him, the sultan wasted no time in talking, beyond remarking that the mere sight of a doctor threw the princess into transports of rage. He then led the prince up to a room under the roof, which had an opening through which he might observe the princess, without himself being seen.

The prince looked and beheld the princess reclining on a sofa, with tears in her eyes, singing softly to herself a song bewailing her sad destiny which had deprived her, perhaps forever, of a being she so tenderly loved. The young man's heart beat fast as he listened, for he needed no further proof that her madness was feigned and that it was love of him which had caused her to resort to this trick. He softly left his hiding place and returned to the sultan, to whom he reported that he was sure from certain signs the princess's malady was not incurable but he must see her and speak with her alone.

The sultan made no difficulty in consenting to this and commanded that he should be ushered in to the princess's apartment The moment she caught sight of his physician's robe, she sprang from her seat in a fury, and heaped insults upon him. The prince took no notice of her behaviour and, aproaching quite close so his words might be heard by her alone, he said in a low whisper, "Look at me, Princess, and you will see that I am no doctor but the Prince of Persia, who has come to set you free."

At the sound of his voice, the Princess of Bengal suddenly grew calm, and an expression of joy overspread her face, such as only comes when what we wish for most and expect the least suddenly happens to us. For some time she was too enchanted to speak, and Prince Firouz Schah took advantage of her silence to explain to her all that had occurred: his despair at watching her disappear before his very eyes, the oath he had sworn to follow her over the world, and his rapture at finally discovering her in the palace at Cashmere. When he had finished, he begged in his turn that the princess would tell him how she had come there, so he might the better devise some means of rescuing her from the tyranny of the sultan.

It needed but a few words from the princess to make him acquainted with the whole situation, and how she had been forced to play the part of a mad woman in order to escape from a marriage with the sultan, who had not had sufficient politeness even to ask her consent. If necessary, she added, she had resolved to die sooner than permit herself to be forced into such a union and so break faith with the prince she loved.

The prince then inquired if she knew what had become of the enchanted horse since the Indian's death, but the princess could only reply that she had heard nothing about it. Still she did not suppose that the horse could have been forgotten by the sultan after all she had told him of its value.

To this the prince agreed, and they consulted together over a plan by which she might be able to make her escape and return with him into Persia. As the first step, she was to dress herself with care and receive the sultan with civility when he visited her next morning.

The sultan was transported with delight on learning the result of the interview, and his opinion of the doctor's skill was raised still higher when, on the following day, the princess behaved toward him in such a way as to persuade him her complete cure would not be long delayed. However he contented himself with assuring her how happy he was to see her health so much improved and exhorted her to make every use of so clever a physician and to repose entire confidence in him. Then he retired, without awaiting any reply from the princess.

The Prince of Persia left the room at the same time and asked if he might be allowed humbly to inquire by what means the Princess of Bengal had reached Cashmere, which was so far distant from her father's kingdom, and how she came to be there alone. The sutltan thought the question very natural and related the same story the Princess of Bengal had told him, adding that he had ordered the enchanted horse to be taken to his treasury as a curiosity, though he was quite ignorant how it could be used.

"Sire," replied the physician, "Your Highness's tale has supplied me with the clue I needed to complete the recovery of the princess. During her voyage hither on an enchanted horse a portion of its enchantment has by some means been communicated to her person, and it can only be dissipated by certain perfumes of which I possess the secret.

"If Your Highness will deign to consent and to give the court and the people one of the most astonishing spectacles they have ever witnessed, command the horse to be brought into the big square outside the palace, and leave the rest to me. I promise that in a very few moments, in the presence of all the assembled multitude, you shall see the princess as healthy both in mind and body as ever she was in her life. And in order to make the spectacle as impressive as possible, I would suggest that she should be richly dressed and covered with the noblest jewels of the crown."

The sultan readily agreed to all the prince proposed, and the following morning he desired that the enchanted horse should be taken from the treasury and brought into the great square of the palace. Soon the rumour began to spread through the town that something extraordinary was about to happen, and such a crowd began to collect that the guards had to be called out to keep order and to make a way for the enchanted horse.

When all was ready the sultan appeared and took his place on a platform, surrounded by the chief nobles and officers of his court. When they were seated the Princess of Bengal was seen leaving the palace, accompanied by the ladies who had been assigned to her by the sultan. She slowly approached the enchanted horse and, with the help of her ladies, mounted on its back. Directly she was in the saddle, with her feet in the stirrups and the bridle in her hand, the physician placed around the horse some large braziers full of burning coals, into each of which he threw a perfume composed of all sorts of delicious scents. Then he crossed his hands over his breast, and with lowered eyes walked three times round the horse, muttering the while certain words.

Soon there arose from the burning braziers a thick smoke which almost concealed both the horse and princess; this was the moment for which the prince had been waiting. Springing lightly up behind the lady, he leaned forward and turned the peg, and as the horse darted up into the air, he cried aloud so that his words were heard by all present, "Sultan of Cashmere, when you wish to marry princesses who have sought your protection, learn first to gain their consent."

It was in this way that the Prince of Persia rescued the Princess of Bengal and returned with her to Persia, where they descended this time before the palace of the king himself. The marriage was only delayed long enough to make the ceremony as brilliant as possible, and as soon as the rejoicings were over, an ambassador was sent to the King of Bengal, to inform him of what had passed and to ask his approbation of the alliance between the two countries, which he heartily gave.

THE COWARDLY LION

Dorothy has been swept up into a tornado and transported to the magical land of Oz. Once in Oz, Dorothy is told that she will find the wizard who can return her to Kansas by following the yellow brick road. As she travels up the road, she meets new friends.

L. FRANK BAUM

All this time Dorothy and her companions had been walking through the thick woods. The road was still paved with yellow brick, but these were much covered by dried branches and dead leaves from the trees and the walking was not at all good.

There were few birds in this part of the forest, for birds love the open country where there is plenty of sunshine, but now and then there came a deep growl from some wild animal hidden among the trees. These sounds made the little girl's heart beat fast, for she did not know what made them; but Toto knew, and he walked close to Dorothy's side, and did not even bark in return.

"How long will it be," the child asked of the Tin Woodman, "before we are out of the forest?"

"I cannot tell," was the answer, "for I have never been to the Emerald City. But my father went there once, when I was a boy, and he said it was a long journey through a dangerous country, although nearer to the city where Oz dwells the country is beautiful. But I am not afraid so long as I have my oil-can, and nothing can hurt the Scarecrow, while you bear upon your forehead the mark of the good Witch's kiss, and that will protect you from harm."

"But Toto!" said the girl, anxiously; "what will protect him?"

"We must protect him ourselves, if he is in danger," replied the Tin Woodman.

Just as he spoke there came from the forest a terrible roar, and the next moment a great Lion bounded into the road. With one blow of his paw he sent the Scarecrow spining over and over to the edge of the road, and then he struck at the Tin Woodman with his sharp claws. But, to the Lion's surprise, he could make no impression on the tin, although the Woodman fell over in the road and lay still.

Little Toto, now that he had an enemy to face, ran barking toward the Lion, and the great beast had opened his mouth to bite the dog, when Dorothy, fearing Toto would be killed, and heedless of danger, rushed forward and slapped the Lion upon his nose as hard as she could, while she cried out:

"Don't you dare to bite Toto! You ought to be ashamed of yourself, a big beast like you, to bite a poor little dog!"

"I didn't bite him" said the Lion, as he rubbed his nose with his paw where Dorothy had hit it.

"No, but you tried to," she retorted. "You are nothing but a big coward."

"I know it," said the Lion, hanging his head in shame; "I've always known it. But how can I help it?"

"I don't know, I'm sure. To think of your striking a stuffed man, like the poor Scarecrow!"

"Is he stuffed?" asked the Lion, in surprise, as he watched her pick up the Scarecrow and set him upon his feet, while she patted him into shape again.

"Of course he's stuffed," replied Dorothy, who was still angry.

"That's why he went over so easily," remarked the Lion. "It astonished me to see him whirl around so. Is the other one stuffed, also?"

"No," said Dorothy, "he's made of tin." And she helped the Woodman up again.

"That's why he nearly blunted my claws," said the Lion. "When they scratched against the tin it made a cold shiver run down my back. What is that little animal you are so tender of?"

"He is my dog, Toto," answered Dorothy.

"Is he made of tin, or stuffed?" asked the Lion.

"Neither. He's a—a—a meat dog," said the girl.

"Oh. He's a curious animal, and seems remarkably small, now that I look at him. No one would think of biting such a little thing except a coward like me," continued the Lion, sadly.

"What makes you a coward?" asked Dorothy, looking at the great beast in wonder, for he was as big as a small horse.

"It's a mystery," replied the Lion. "I suppose I was born that way. All the other animals in the forest naturally expect me to be brave, for the Lion is everywhere thought to be the King of Beasts. I learned that if I roared very loudly every living thing was frightened and got out of my way. Whenever I've met a man I've been awfully scared; but I just roared at him, and he has always run away as fast as he could go. If the elephants and the tigers and the bears had ever tried to fight me I should have run myself—I'm such a coward; but just as soon as they hear me roar they

all try to get away from me, and of course I let them go."

"But that isn't right. The King of Beasts shouldn't be a coward," said the Scarecrow.

"I know it," returned the Lion, wiping a tear from his eye with the tip of his tail; "it is my great sorrow, and makes my life very unhappy. But whenever there is danger my heart begins to beat fast."

"Perhaps you have heart disease," said the Tin Woodman.

"It may be," said the Lion.

"If you have," continued the Tin Woodman, "you ought to be glad, for it proves you have a heart. For my part, I have no heart; so I cannot have heart disease."

"Perhaps," said the Lion, thoughtfully, "if I had no heart I should not be a coward."

"Have you brains?" asked the Scarecrow.

"I suppose so. I've never looked to see," replied the Lion.

"I am going to the great Oz to ask him to give me some," remarked the Scarecrow, "for my head is stuffed with straw."

"And I am going to ask him to give me a heart," said the Woodman.

"And I am going to ask him to send Toto and me back to Kansas," added Dorothy.

"Do you think Oz could give me courage?" asked the Cowardly Lion.

"Just as easily as he could give me brains," said the Scarecrow.

"Or give me a heart," said the Tin Woodman.

"Or send me back to Kansas," said Dorothy.

"Then, if you don't mind, I'll go with you," said the Lion, "for my life is simply unbearable without a bit of courage."

"You will be very welcome," answered Dorothy, "for you will help to keep away the other wild beasts. It seems to me they must be more cowardly than you are if they allow you to scare them so easily."

"They really are," said the Lion; "but that doesn't make me any braver, and as long as I know myself to be a coward I shall be unhappy."

So once more the little company set off upon the journey, the Lion walking with stately strides at Dorothy's side. Toto did not approve this new comrade at first, for he could not forget how nearly he had been crushed between the Lion's great jaws; but after a time he became more at ease, and presently Toto and the Cowardly Lion had grown to be good friends.

During the rest of that day there was no other adventure to mar the peace of their journey. Once, indeed, the Tin Woodman stepped upon a beetle that was crawling along the road, and killed the poor little thing. This made the Tin Woodman very unhappy, for he was always careful not to hurt any living creature; and as he walked along he wept several tears of sorrow and regret. These tears ran slowly down his face and over the hinges of his jaw, and there they rusted. When Dorothy presently asked him a question the Tin Woodman could not open his mouth, for his jaws were tightly rusted together. He became greatly frightened at this and made many motions to Dorothy to relieve him, but she could not understand. The Lion was also puzzled to know what was wrong. But the Scarecrow seized the oil-can from Dorothy's basket and oiled the Woodman's jaws, so that after a few moments he could talk as well as before.

"This will serve me a lesson," said he, "to look where I step. For if I should kill another bug or beetle I should surely cry again, and crying rusts my jaw so that I cannot speak."

Thereafter he walked very carefully, with his eyes on the road, and when he saw a tiny ant toiling by he would step over it, so as not to harm it. The Tin Woodman knew very well he had no heart, and therefore he took great care never to be cruel or unkind to anything.

"You people with hearts," he said, "have something to guide you, and need never do wrong; but I have no heart, and so I must be very careful. When Oz gives me a heart of course I needn't mind so much."

ACKNOWLEDGEMENTS

Care has been taken to ensure that all of the material contained herein is in the public domain. If any of the material contained herein is not in the public domain the publishers will gladly receive any information that will enable them to rectify any reference or credit line in subsequent editions.

"The Great Sea Serpent" by Hans Christian Andersen. From *The Complete Fairy Tales and Stories of Hans Christian Andersen* by Hans Christian Andersen.

"All Gone" by Walter de la Mare. From *Animal Stories* by Walter de la Mare.

"The Beginning of the Armadilloes" by Rudyard Kipling. From *Just So Stories* by Rudyard Kipling, © 1902.

"The Monkey and the Jelly-fish" by Andrew Lang. From *The Violet Fairy Book* by Andrew Lang, © 1901.

"The Last of the Dragons" by E. Nesbitt. From *The Complete Book of Dragons*.

"Babe, the Blue Ox" by Esther Shepard. From *Paul Bunyan* by Esther Shepard, © 1924.

"The Raven and the Goose" by Knud Rasmussen, translated by W. Worster. From *Eskimo Folk-Tales* by Knud Rasmussen, translated by W. Worster, © 1921.

"The Fire-bird, the Horse of Power and the Princess Vasilissa" by Arthur Ransome. From *Old Peter's Russian Tales* by Arthur Ransome, © 1916.

"How the Rabbit Lost his Tail" by Cyrus Macmillan. From *Canadian Wonder Tales* by Cyrus Macmillan, © 1918.

"How Some Wild Animals Became Tame Ones" by Andrew Lang. From *The Orange Fairy Book* by Andrew Lang.

"The Reluctant Dragon" by Kenneth Grahame. From *Dream Days* by Kenneth Grahame, © 1898.

"The Cat Who Became Head-forester" by Arthur Ransome. From *Old Peter's Russian Tales* by Arthur Ransome, © 1916.

"The Mock Turtle's Story" by Lewis Carroll. From *Alice's Adventures in Wonderland* by Lewis Carroll.

"The Two Frogs" by Andrew Lang. From *The Violet Fairy Book* by Andrew Lang, © 1901.

"The Dance of the Royal Ants" by Alice Gall and Fleming Crew. From *The Little Black Ant* by Alice Gall and Fleming Crew, © 1936.

"Tale of a Tortoise and of a Mischievous Monkey" by Andrew Lang. From *The Brown Fairy Book* by Andrew Lang, © 1904.

"The Enchanted Horse" by Andrew Lang. From *The Arabian Nights' Entertainment* by Andrew Lang, © 1898.

"The Cowardly Lion" by L. Frank Baum. From *The Wonderful Wizard of Oz* by L. Frank Baum, © 1899.